Sherlock Holmes and
The Terrible Secret

As related from the case notes of

Dr. John H. Watson M.D.

Fred Thursfield

Paperback ISBN 978-1-78092-228-7
ePub ISBN 978-1-78092-229-4
PDF ISBN 978-1-78092-230-0

Published in the UK by MX Publishing
335 Princess Park Manor, Royal Drive, London, N11 3GX
www.mxpublishing.com

Cover design by
www.staunch.com

Prologue

The Triangle Shirtwaist Factory fire in New York City America on March 25, 1911, was the deadliest industrial disaster in the history of the city and resulted in the fourth highest loss of life from an industrial accident in American history. The fire caused the deaths of 146 workers, all who died from the fire, smoke inhalation, or falling to their deaths. Most of the victims were recent Jewish and Italian immigrant women aged sixteen to twenty-three; the oldest victim was 48, the youngest were two fourteen-year-old girls. Because the managers had locked the doors to the stairwells and exits – a common practice at the time to prevent pilferage and unauthorized breaks – many of the workers who could not escape the burning building jumped to their death from the eighth, ninth, and tenth floors to the streets below.

As terrible as this disaster was, with the emotional impact it had on family friends and society was devastating. In three years there would be a much larger and worse tragedy to come.

London, November 1914

Chapter 1

On 28th June 1914 Archduke Franz Ferdinand, the heir to the Austro-Hungarian throne, and his wife Sophie, were assassinated during a state visit to Sarajevo, the capital of the Austro-Hungarian province of Bosnia-Herzegovina. The fatal shots were fired by nineteen year old Gavrilo Princip, a Bosnian Serb who wanted Bosnian unification with Serbia and independence from the Austro-Hungarian Empire.

Franz Ferdinand, as a member of the ruling Habsburg family, was a symbol of that ancient, multi national empire and a repression of it minorities. Unknown to his assassin, the archduke, who was an advocate of political reform, had recently given an after dinner toast…

"To peace…what would we get out of war with Serbia? We'd lose the lives of young men and we'd spend money better used elsewhere, what would we gain for heavens sake? A few plum trees, a pasture full of goat droppings, and a bunch of rebellious killers."

There had been many major changes since Holmes and I had solved our most recent case together; on a global scale because of a catalyst in the form of an assignation of royalty six months earlier on June 28 in Sarajevo Bosnia.

The world had now been plunged into a war on a scale that never before could have been imagined or had ever been witnessed. The resulting conflict would bring decades of simmering unrest and social reform to a boil it would arbitrarily erase old countries and create new ones.

There were also changes on a more personal level. I was starting to notice that as the year was drawing to a close there was a noticeable and perceptible lack of interest and commitment from Holmes. He showed very little interest in the few cases we were pursuing.

I would see him seated in his favorite chair and instead of scouring the news papers looking for some hint of crime he was in fact intensely perusing books with titles like Cheshire's Bees and Bee-keeping, A.J. Cook's, The Bee-Keepers' Guide; or Manual of the Apiary and the 1910 Bee Keeper Review edited by W.Z. Hutchinson.

Puzzled I casually asked in passing what had prompted his change in reading material and why bee keeping in particular? Holmes looked up from his latest tome and answered "I am an omnivorous reader with a strangely retentive memory for trifles. Education never ends Watson. It is a series of lessons, with the greatest for the last."

When I thought back on some of the more memorable cases we shared and solved together recently including The Blue Carbuncle – The Cracked Mirror – The Dead Mans Switch – The Discarded Cigarette - The False Wall – The Gold Ring – The Jade Broach – The Open Door and The Stopped Clock I found myself trying to formulate a polite way to ask my friend if he was indeed contemplating a change of career.

After all Holmes was a man of habits... and I had become one of them... a comrade... upon whose nerve he could place some reliance... a whetstone for his mind. I stimulated him. If I irritated him by a certain methodical slowness in my mentality, that irritation served only to make his own flame-like intuitions and impressions flash up the more vividly and swiftly. Such was my humble role in our alliance…an alliance I very much wanted to continue.

The answer to this problem that was constantly in the back of my mind was resolved after dinner at home one evening. I was settling in my favorite chair in our parlor with my pipe, tobacco and prescription book in my lap. I was writing out medication orders for patients that I would see the next day during my rounds at the hospital when the telephone (invented in 1876) in our front entrance began to ring.

Thinking it might be the hospital calling about a particular patient I started to rise from my chair to take the call when Mary passed by saying "John I'll answer it." It only rang twice more when I heard the receiver lift and her voice say into the device "Hello?"

I must stop my narrative here for a moment.

Of all the people that have entered into my chronicles about Holmes cases there is one who is briefly mentioned from time to time...usually only as "Mary my wife". This reference is only done (at best) in passing. But I think that after all of this time I may have done her an injustice. As she does play a pivotal role in this case it is time to properly introduce my wife to my readers.

Mary Watson nee Morstan was born in the Andaman Islands India in 1869, her father was a captain of a large Indian Regiment, her mother the head and matron of a large household. In 1878 her father disappeared in mysterious circumstances that would later be proved to be related to the mystery in The Sign of Four.

Her mother died soon after her birth and as she had no other relatives in England she was sent to live with and receive an education (in accordance with the received wisdom of the time about children in the colony of India.) with close friends of the family. It was an interesting turn of events that Mary and I are first introduced in The Sign of Four; she had hired Holmes at the time while she had been making a living as a governess.

Mary and I become attracted to each other, and it was a case of love at first sight. However, it was only after the case was resolved that was I able to propose to her.
So that you have a better image when she is referred to in this narrative I shall now describe my wife the first time we were introduced by Holmes.

Mary Morstan (at the time) was foremost confident, assured yet a warm and personable woman. She was a bit shorter than me, of slight build, fine features, long curly dark chestnut brown hair, deep emerald green eyes and an infectious smile.

Her soft lilting voice captured my heart with our first meeting. I can still recall how I felt when she said "Hello Dr. Watson, it is a pleasure to meet you."

Now I shall bring the reader back to the present moment. Although I could only hear one side of the long distance exchange of words I could tell by the rising level of concern in my wife's voice that she was not receiving good news. The conversation ended with a some what distraught "I will tell him Mrs. Hudson…good bye."

When she hung up the receiver she returned to the parlor. Mary nervously stood before me for a moment not quite sure how to repeat the contents of the telephone conversation she had just had. When she saw me look up from my prescription book she announced "that was Mrs. Hudson John ; Sherlock (I will explain later in the narrative as to how my wife comes to call my friend by his first name) has informed her that he wishes to meet with both of you tomorrow afternoon in his rooms. Sensing my obvious question she continued "Mrs. Hudson wasn't told about the nature and purpose of the meeting, only that it was imperative for you and her to be in attendance."

Chapter 2

Some of the opening encounters of the war were not unlike those seen in previous European conflicts. The initial rapid advances covered hundreds of miles and were made by cavalry armed with lances and dressed in bright uniforms more suitable for parade days. The world of 1914 was a mixture of old and new. Horse drawn carts were gradually replaced with automobiles, electricity was spreading beyond the cities; telephones were making an appearance in better off homes.

Military technology had also undergone a substantial leap in recent years. Powerful new artillery, poison gas, airplanes and later on tanks made their first appearance in this war. Yet at its start even the most seasoned military men could not predict which of this new weaponry would play an important role in the conflict, nor could imagine the destructive power of mass produced weapons that were now available.

I wasn't quite sure if I could find the time from my now very busy hospital duties to fulfill my friend's request. Even during the short time we had been in a state of war the number of wounded (including soldiers, pilots, sailors and civilians) being received at St Bartholomew's never seemed to end.

The wounds both physical and psychological I witnessed on the soldiers who were returning from the front were deeper and far more ghastly than any I had witnessed in all my time serving as an army doctor in Afghanistan.

I felt helpless while I witnessed daily an emotionally and spiritually demoralizing grey winters scene unfold in the hospital court yard of wounded, bandaged and field dressed young boys being off loaded on canvas cots from the back of army ambulances then taken by stretcher bearers into the hospital to be mended as best we could.

No amount of medical training or experience could ever prepare you to deal with the new, vast and inhuman weapons that were now being used in combat and their surgical like effects on the men these new eradicating tools were being used upon.

In addition to nursing visible wounds we were now treating what for the most part was an invisible poorly understood injury. What the soldiers coming back from the battle called "shell shock" Many senior figures military, political and civil, simply refused to admit it existed, preferring to believe suffers were cowards or, in a phrase commonly used, "lacking moral fiber."

We saw shell shock become manifest in many ways, from comparatively mild regular panic attacks to the severest forms in which men were reduced to twitching wrecks or ended up in a catatonic state.

I was trying to keep busy so as to not think about the subject or matter that was no doubt going to be brought up with me and Mrs. Hudson. Before I knew it my morning hospital rounds were completed and it was now mid day. I now found myself warmly dressed in my hat; coat and foot wear bravely standing outside at the very cold West Smithfield entrance of the hospital hailing a motor taxi to take me to 221B Baker Street.

After settling in, and giving the driver directions after a short ride I was again facing a familiar door that I had known for many years both as a lodger and as a guest. Not sure as to what to expect I knocked and waited for Mrs. Hudson to open it. When the door opened I tried to get a sounding of Mrs. Hudson's expression or mood to prepare myself for what was coming.

After entering and removing my seasonal outer wear in unusual silence I noticed there was a troubling absence of the friendly casual back and forth banter that would have normally passed between us as I was being lead through the house.

"He is waiting for us Dr. Watson" was all Mrs. Hudson said solemnly as she made her way to the carpeted stairs that led up to Holmes rooms.

Quietly following her up the 17 stairs any one would have mistaken the unfolding scene more as a funeral procession than merely as a guest politely following a land lady. We crossed the threshold and saw that Holmes was already comfortably seated in his parlor with his back to us.

As we came around into his view…he silently gestured towards the other unoccupied chair on his right and the love seat on his left as our places to be seated.

When Mrs. Hudson and I sat down Holmes dramatically rose (like an actor given an off stage cue) from where he had been seated and walked with his hands behind his back over to the winter frost edged windows that looked down onto the late afternoon.

Snow was softly settling on Baker Street and he took a moment to observe the parade of humanity and commerce that regularly happens by at this time each day.

The scene he had witnessed so many times from this second story vantage point had been slowly and almost imperceptibly changing during the years of his residency at 221B Baker Street. What he now witnessed was only one of many reasons for the decision he was about to reveal. It was as if the events of past July had put a very different and unsettling perspective on familiar sights.

Where there had been only a mix of pedestrians, shoppers and wheeled street traffic. Now there was the occasional presence of men wearing dark khaki serge winter military uniforms walking in highly polished black military boots.

Before the war there had been unobstructed views of places of business, commerce and government affairs. This had been replaced with walls of sand bags the height of the ground floor. Tan colored sand filled burlap bags piled and staggered on top of each other in front of important buildings offering some protection against explosive attacks.

When Holmes thought that he could come to accept these changes then he sighted the occasional brightly colored recruiting poster of Lord Kitchener pointing at passers by extolling Britons to join the countries army. These were prominently displayed in a shop or public house at street level reminding Holmes how much the world had changed.

In 1914, at the start of the First World War, Lord Kitchener became Secretary of State for War, a Cabinet Minister. One of the few men to foresee a long war, one in which Britain's victory was far from secure, he organized the largest volunteer army that Britain, and indeed the Empire, had seen. He also commissioned a significant expansion of materials production to fight Germany on the Western Front. His commanding image, appearing on recruiting posters demanding "Your country needs you! "

Defence of the Realm Act of 1914

The Defence of the Realm Act (DORA) of 1914 governed all lives in Britain during World War One. The Defence of the Realm Act was added to as the war progressed and it listed everything that people were not allowed to do in time of war. As World War one evolved, so DORA evolved. The first version of the Defence of the Realm Act was introduced on August 8th 1914. This stated that:

No-one was allowed to talk about naval or military matters in public places

No-one was allowed to spread rumours about military matters

No-one was allowed to buy binoculars

No-one was allowed to trespass on railway lines or bridges

No-one was allowed to melt down gold or silver

No-one was allowed to light bonfires or fireworks

No-one was allowed to give bread to horses, horses or chickens

No-one was allowed to use invisible ink when writing abroad

No-one was allowed to buy brandy or whisky in a railway refreshment room

No-one was allowed to ring church bells

The government could take over any factory or workshop

The government could try any civilian breaking these laws

The government could take over any land it wanted to

The government could censor newspapers

As the war continued and evolved, the government introduced more acts to DORA. The government introduced British Summer Time to give more daylight for extra work. Opening hours in pubs were cut beer was watered down customers in pubs were not allowed to buy a round of drinks

The Home Front during World War One refers to life in Britain during the war itself. The Home Front saw a massive change in the role of women, rationing, the bombing of parts of Britain by the Germans (the first time civilians were targeted in war) conscientious objectors and strikes by discontented workers. The whole nation was under the jurisdiction of DORA (Defence of the Realm Act).

BY THE KING

A PROCLAMATION FOR CALLING OUT THE ARMY RESERVE AND EMBODYING THE TERRITORIAL FORCE

GEORGE R.I.

WHEREAS by the Reserve Forces Act, 1882, it is amongst Other things enacted that in case of imminent national danger or of great emergency it shall be lawful for Us by Proclamation, the occasion having first been communicated to Parliament, to order that the Army Reserve shall be called out on permanent service; and by any such Proclamation to order a Secretary of State from time to time to give and when given to revoke or vary such directions as may seem necessary or proper for calling out the forces or force mentioned in the Proclamation or all or any of the men belonging thereto :

And Whereas the present state of public affairs and the extent of the demands on Our Military Forces for the protection of the interests of the Empire do in Our opinion constitute a case of great emergency within the meaning of the said Act, and We have communicated the same to Parliament :

And Whereas by the Territorial and Reserve Forces Act, 1907, it is, amongst other things, enacted that immediately upon and by virtue of the issue of a Proclamation ordering the Army Reserve to be called out on permanent service it shall be lawful for Us to order Our Army Council

from time to time to give and when given to revoke or vary such directions as may seem necessary or proper for embodying all or any part of the Territorial Force,

and in particular to make such special arrangements as they think proper with regard to units or individuals whose services may be required in other than a Military capacity :

Now, Therefore, We do in pursuance of the Reserve Forces Act, 1882, hereby order that Our Army Reserve be called out on permanent service, and We do hereby order the Right Honourable HERBERT HENRY ASQUITH, one of Our Principal Secretaries of State, from time to time to give and when given to revoke or vary such directions as may seem necessary or proper for calling out Our Army Reserve or all or any of the men belonging thereto : And We do hereby further order Our Army Council from time to time to give and when given to revoke or vary such directions as may seem necessary or proper for embodying all or any part of the Territorial Force, and in particular to make such special arrangements as they think proper with regard to units or individuals whose services may be required in other than a Military capacity.

Given at Our Court at Buckingham Palace this Fourth day of August, in the year of our Lord One thousand nine hundred and fourteen, and in the Fifth year of Our Reign At the Court at Buckingham Palace, the 4th day of August 1914.

God save the King

Number 10 Downing Street

Owing to the summary rejection by the German Government of the request made by His Majesty's Government for assurances that the neutrality of Belgium would be respected, His Majesty's Ambassador in Berlin has received his passport, and His Majesty's Government has declared to the German Government that a state of war exists between Great Britain and Germany as from 11pm on August 4th."

A united nation since only 1871, Germany was now the rising force of Europe, ruled by the ambitious Kaiser Wilhelm, Germany formed an alliance with the much older empire of Austria Hungary. Together these central powers now dominated the heart of Europe.

When war was declared in August 1914, there were street celebrations throughout the length and breadth of Great Britain. Such scenes were repeated throughout Europe. Many believed that the war would be over by Christmas 1914 and many young men rushed to answer the call to arms - as did many men who were too old to serve but wanted to show their patriotism.

People began thinking of what might be ahead. On the streets reservists could be seen every where. It seemed as if people were ready to fight the world at the drop of a hat...a new army recruit, London

The government asked for 100,000 volunteers but got 750,000 in just one month. The public was quickly deluged with numerous propaganda posters to encourage everyone in their nation's time of need.

Those who did not want to join the military could be targeted by people as cowards - being handed white feathers and being refused service by shops and pubs etc. Many believed that victory against Germany - and a quick one at that - was a certainty and the vast bulk of the nation was supportive not only of the declaration of war but also of any man who wanted to join up.

The demand for war munitions meant that factories worked all but round the clock to ensure that soldiers were well supplied with ammunition. This invariably led to accidents as safety was sometimes seen as secondary to producing munitions.

The worst factory accident was at Silverton in the East End of London. On January 19th, 1917, the munitions factory exploded and 69 people were killed and over 400 injured. Extensive damage was done to the area around the factory. In all, a total of 1,500 civilians were killed during the war.

"There were shouts of "fire", well you could not miss it, and the whole place was lit up. We were all outside looking. I went upstairs to get a shawl. Suddenly I was downstairs and the house was on top of me. It's funny but I can't really remember hearing the explosion.....our house was blown down right enough.

We don't go up to Silverton again....I didn't go to school again. There was no school, no house, so there was no point."

Mabel Bastable, an eye-witness at Silverton

I could tell by his posture as he was standing in front of the window that Holmes was composing his thoughts…for a moment I almost heard him softly utter the words "Well, Watson; we seem to have fallen upon evil days. I shall not miss any of this."

Turning to face both of us a smile briefly passed his lips and he started "so to the matter of why we are all here." Then like a seasoned actor starting to recite a dramatic monologue he began:

"The world as I knew and understood it does not exist for me any more. Recent European conflicts and the world of criminal activity (well) there is nothing new under the sun. It has all been done before.

The scale of one has grown larger, more complex, and involved and not easily understood while the other has grown smaller and no longer presents any real or stimulating challenges for me. "My mind," he said, "rebels at stagnation. "

"Give me problems, give me work, give me the most abstruse cryptogram or the most intricate analysis, and I am in my own proper atmosphere. I can dispense then with artificial stimulants. But I abhor the dull routine of existence. I crave for mental exaltation.

That is why I have chosen my own particular profession, or rather created it, for I am the only one in the world"

"On the second point you fully know and understand Watson that I cannot live without brain-work. What else is there to live for?" then as if to emphasize the last part of this thought Holmes said with a small amount of frustration in his voice "Even I cannot make bricks without clay."

"The emotional qualities are antagonistic to clear reasoning. I assure you that the most winning woman I ever knew was hanged for poisoning three little children for their insurance-money, and the most repellent man of my acquaintance is a philanthropist who has spent nearly a quarter of a million upon the London poor.

In the end it all comes down to a case of I just listen to their story, they listen to my comments, and then I pocket my fee" and with that he returned to his chair and sat back down. Then to finish while seated Holmes sighed cynically and concluded with "it is now a matter that a client is to me a mere unit, only a factor in a problem."

Not quite sure if this broad statement was in any way connected with Holmes latest choice of reading material I blindly inquired "Where, or should I say what do you intend to focus your interests on then?"

"Bee keeping" replied Holmes calmly as he picked up a related book that was near to him. "I intend to retire some time soon to a modest cottage in Doncaster where I intend to take up the hobby of beekeeping as my primary occupation.

I may eventually even turn my hand to write the occasional treatise on bee culture (here another brief smile passed Holmes lips) with some observations upon segregation of the queen. This was no doubt the one final and subtle reference to my long standing habit of keeping a journal of Holmes cases.

To acquaint the reader as to Holmes new place of residence: Doncaster is a town in South Yorkshire and the principal settlement of the Metropolitan Borough of Doncaster. The town is about 20 miles from Sheffield and is popularly referred to as "Donny". The distance from Doncaster to London is about 151 miles South by rail.

During the Industrial Revolution the railway came to Doncaster, and the Great Northern Railway established the Doncaster Locomotive and Carriage Building Works. The reasons for this were Doncaster's communication links, the necessity to transport coal quickly and efficiently and Doncaster's expertise in specialist metal products. An extensive housing program was undertaken for the increased population.

The Chairman of the Great Northern, anxious about the workers and their families' spiritual welfare, persuaded the directors to contribute towards the building of St. James' Church, which became known as the "Plant Church". The railway also built St. James' School.

There was a long and very uncomfortable silence that followed Holmes profound statement, then Mrs. Hudson putting her emotions to one side asked in a very practical tone of voice that of a land lady merely addressing a tenant "when do you plan to vacate your rooms Mr. Holmes?" Seeing the impact his statement had made on her he hoped his soothing answer would be some what reassuring

"Not until the trees in Regents Park have grown new leaves Mrs. Hudson."

August 10 France.

In accordance with a strategic blue print for war against Germany known as Plan XVII, Frances army of Alsace under General Paul Pau advances against the German held city of Mulhouse in Alsace, heralding a series of battles along the French and Belgium borders.

Western Front the first of Liege's 12 forts falls to the Germans following a pounding by 17 in howitzers brought up by Second Army Commander General Karl von Bulow.

August 12 Britain the government declares war on Austria Hungary.

August 12 – 21 Balkans Advancing across the border into Serbia from the North and the North West, some 200, 000 Austro Hungarian troops led by General Oskar Potiorck invade. Although out numbered, the Serbians forces under Marshal Radomir Putnik put up stout resistance during the battle of the Jadar River, forcing the invaders to begin with drawing by August 16.

August 14 the novelist H.G. Wells (The Time Machine) calls the conflict "The war to end all wars."

Chapter 3

By December 1915 the Eastern Front between Russia and the two Central Powers, Germany and Austria, Hungary stretched from the Baltic to Romania. It was twice the length of the Western Front and the character of the warfare was very different.

There were huge logistical problems, with vast distances connected by slow trains and poor roads, all compounded by the relative industrial backwardness of Russia and Austria, Hungary. In contrast to the static fighting in Belgium and France, where the line would not alter by more than twenty miles in the following three years there were opportunities here for maneuver and mobility.

The weeks that lead up to Christmas were surprisingly uneventful. The worst of the December snow storms had finally passed. I was attending to less war related injuries at the hospital. Which I believed meant that other than wounds received from the occasional sniper attack it was probably far too cold to wage any real warfare by troops going "over the top".

The soldiers on both sides would for relative comfort and safety be firmly dug into trenches for the duration. These two sets of now frozen man made ditches ran the collective length of the continent from the North Sea down to the Ionian and Aegean Sea

"In those days your brain – what shall I say – wasn't developed enough to realize what war was and everybody said it would be over by Christmas. Now Christmas came and it wasn't"...a soldier at the front.

This tactical stalemate had for all intents and purposes divided the continent into roughly two halves with France and Italy on the western side of the German Empire, the Austrian Hungarian Empire and the Turkish Empire on the eastern side, this would be come to be known as the Western Front.

Mary and I had from the onset of war had decided that despite events going on across the English Channel we would continue to celebrate the festive season as we always had since spending our first Christmas together as a married couple.

This meant my wife spent a few happy hours finding the many boxes of festive decorations we owned and transforming our downstairs into a bright and colorful reflection of what this time should be about and not what we were facing.

My primary duty at this time was to secure a suitable Christmas tree for our parlor, a much enjoyed tradition in England which had been started by Queen Victoria's consort and husband Prince Albert in 1841 no matter what…this task always put me in the festive spirit.

Our tradition continued, once bringing the tree home I secured it in its stand then I placed white candles on each of the branches in such a way that the carefully placed candle when lit would not ignite the branch above.

I would then let Mary place the many hand made decorations' on the ever green tree; I am the first to admit she had a much better hand at it than I did. Although our home had been illuminated by electric light for some time there were occasions during the festive season when we wanted to spend time together with just the light from the many candles glowing softly on each branch of our now decorated tree.

Last was the wrapping of the garland around the tree which had always been a collaborative effort, Mary wrapping the lower part of the now decorated tree and me the remaining upper branches.

My secondary duty had grown out of concern as to how my friend would spend Christmas Day. I had it on good authority that Mrs. Hudson left 221B Baker Street early to spend the day with her family leaving Holmes alone in quiet solitude.

It had initially been Mary herself who had suggested inviting Holmes to share the special day with us. The first time I had brought up the subject during one of my ever increasing rare visits I had expected the offer to be scoffed at then rejected. I have to admit though that his surprising positive acceptance came out of an observation I had made during the Adventure of the Three Garridebs.

I had been superficially wounded. It was worth a wound; it was worth many wounds; to know the depth of loyalty and love which lay behind that cold mask. Holmes clear, hard eyes were dimmed for a moment, and the firm lips were shaking.

For the one and only time I caught a glimpse of a great heart as well as of a great brain. All my years of humble but single-minded service culminated in that moment of revelation.

So now every Christmas day at around 2:00 p.m. a motor taxi stops in front 126 Hill House Road, a familiar figure bearing a gift under his left coat arm gets out from the left passenger side and makes his way carefully up the snow covered path to our threshold and we both warmly welcome Holmes to share this day with us.

I remember the first Christmas as formal introductions were being made just after Mary's and my wedding. I started to use the familiar (to me) way I had always addressed my friend as part of the introduction to my wife. But somehow I could see that she wouldn't think it proper to be so personal and would feel uncomfortable to use "Holmes" when addressing my friend

Holmes sensing my immediate social dilemma and Mary's discomfort perceptively eased the situation by serenely stating "My brother Mycroft addresses me as Sherlock and you may too."

When the introductions went the other way. I wasn't sure if I should use my wife's first name or stay with the more traditional "Mrs. Watson" Mary no doubt following Holmes relaxed attitude towards names in introductions stated "Our close friends know me as Mary and it would please me if you would address me the same way."

To those who have not met the mentioned brother, Mycroft Holmes is the elder brother (by seven years) of Sherlock Holmes.

Possessing inductive powers exceeding even those of his younger brother, Mycroft is nevertheless incapable of performing detective work similar to that of Holmes. He has never been willing to put in the physical effort necessary to bring cases to their conclusion.

He (Mycroft) has no ambition and no energy. He will not even go out of his way to verify his own solutions, and would rather be considered wrong than take the trouble to prove himself right.

Again and again Holmes has taken a problem to him, and has received an explanation which has afterwards proved to be the correct one. And yet he (Mycroft) was absolutely incapable of working out the practical points.

When I first heard of Mycroft I was told that the older brother audits books for some government departments, Holmes later reveals that Mycroft's true role is more substantial. I was never sure of what Mycroft Holmes' exact position was in the British government; my friend would only comment that "Occasionally he *is* the British government the most indispensable man in the country."

He apparently serves as a sort of human computer: The conclusions of every department are passed to him, and he is the central exchange, the clearinghouse, which makes out the balance. All other men are specialists, but his specialism is omniscience.

Chapter 4

Count Ferdinand Zeppelin, a German army officer, began developing his ideas on airships in 1897. The first Zeppelin flew on 2nd July 1900. The LZ-3 Zeppelin was accepted into army service in March 1909. By the start of the First World War the German Army had seven military Zeppelins. The Zeppelin developed in 1914 could reach a maximum speed of 90 mph and reach a height of 4,750 feet. The Zeppelin had five machine-guns and could carry 4,400 lbs. of bombs.

1915 …

January…2 Zeppelin navel airships each 570 feet long flew over the east coast of England and bombed great Yarmouth and King's Lynn.

January 8: Germany forms a southern army to support the faltering Austrians.

February 4: Germany declares submarine blockade of Britain, with all approaching ships
considered targets. This is the start of Unrestricted Submarine Warfare

March 11: The Reprisals Order, Britain bans all 'neutral' parties from trading with
Germany

April 22: The first use of Poison Gas on the Western Front, in a German attack on Canadian
troops at Ypres. The German Army had 168 tons of chlorine deployed in 5,730 cylinders opposite Langemark-Poelkapelle, north of Ypres.

At 17:30 (5:30 p.m.), in a slight easterly breeze, the gas was released, forming a gray-green cloud that drifted across positions held by French Colonial troops from Martinique who broke ranks, abandoning their trenches and creating an 8,000-yard gap in the Allied line.

However, the German infantry were also wary of the gas and lacking reinforcements, failed to exploit the break before the 1st Canadian Division and assorted French troops reformed the line in scattered, hastily prepared positions 1,000 to 3,000 yards apart.

The Entente governments quickly claimed the attack was a flagrant violation of international law, but Germany argued that the Hague treaty had only banned chemical shells, rather than the use of gas projectors.

In what became the Second Battle of Ypres, the Germans used gas on three more occasions; on 24 April against the 1st Canadian Division, on 2 May near Mouse Trap Farm and on 5 May against the British at Hill 60.

The British Official History stated that at Hill 60, 90 men died from gas poisoning in the trenches or before they could be got to a dressing station; of the 207 brought to the nearest dressing stations, 46 died almost immediately and 12 after long suffering.

Chlorine was a powerful irritant that could inflict damage to the eyes, nose, throat and lungs. At high concentrations and prolonged exposure it could cause death by asphyxiation.

April 25: The Allied ground assault begins in Gallipoli. Lowestoft (Suffolk) and Yarmouth (Norfolk) raided by German battle cruiser squadron.

The Gallipoli Campaign, also known as the Dardanelles Campaign or the Battle of Gallipoli took place at the peninsula of Gallipoli in the Ottoman Empire between 25 April 1915 and 9 January 1916. A joint British and French operation was mounted to capture the Ottoman capital of Istanbul (referred to as 'Constantinople' by Western nations) and secure a sea route to Russia.

The attempt failed, with heavy casualties on both sides. The campaign was considered one of the greatest victories of the Turks and was reflected on as a major failure by the Allies. The campaign was the first major battle undertaken by the Australian and New Zealand Army Corps (ANZAC), and is often considered to mark the birth of national consciousness in both of these countries

May 7:   The Lusitania is sunk by a German submarine; casualties include 124 Americans.

On May 1, 1915, the ship departed New York City bound for Liverpool. Unknown to her passengers but probably no secret to the Germans, almost all her hidden cargo consisted of munitions and contraband destined for the British war effort.

As the fastest ship afloat, the luxurious liner felt secure in the belief she could easily outdistance any submarine. Nonetheless, the menace of submarine attack reduced her passenger list to only half her capacity. On May 7, the ship neared the coast of Ireland.

At 2:10 in the afternoon a torpedo fired by the German submarine U 20 slammed into her side. A mysterious second explosion ripped the liner apart.

Chaos reigned. The ship listed so badly and quickly that lifeboats crashed into passengers crowded on deck, or dumped their loads into the water. Most passengers never had a chance. Within 18 minutes the giant ship slipped beneath the sea. One thousand one hundred nineteen of the 1,924 aboard died. The dead included 124 Americans.

"The Lusitania is a god send to the British. It's quite the most stupid thing the Germans could have done"... a captain in the Royal navy.

The sinking enraged American public opinion. The political fallout was immediate. President Wilson protested strongly to the Germans. Secretary of State William Jennings Bryan, a pacifist, resigned. In September, the Germans announced that passenger ships would be sunk only with prior warning and appropriate safeguards for passengers. However, the seeds of American animosity towards Germany were sown. Within two years America declared war.

May 8: On Saturday afternoon I received a brief telegram at home stating that Homes had finally vacated his rooms 221 B Baker Street (no doubt to a very distraught Mrs. Hudson). After a short train journey (starting at Kings Cross Station on the Great Northern Railway) he had taken up occupancy of his modest cottage (as he referred to it) in South Yorkdale, Doncaster.

In later sporadic letters Holmes would go on to describe his new home which was locally known as "the Beeches". How the cottage appeared from the main road…what the interior rooms both down stairs and upstairs looked like…and most importantly that the spacious back garden contained a number of active and productive bee hives.

As with other transitions I wondered which direction Holmes personal life would now go in. While he may have had the occasional falling out with Mrs. Hudson about one or another aspect of his personal habits she brought order, regularity, sense, good health and direction to his life while he was her lodger.

Other than times when I feared that Holmes might resort to his solution when the tide of his life was low I knew while rooming at 221B Baker Street physically he was being well looked after as any Scottish land lady could.

I speculated that Holmes moving to a country or rural setting might bring back his more "bohemian" habits and lifestyle, with no apparent regard for contemporary standards of tidiness or good order. Although as always in his methods of thought he was the neatest and most methodical of mankind.

But he kept his cigars in the coal-scuttle, his tobacco in the toe end of a Persian slipper, and his unanswered correspondence (including my soon to be unanswered telegraph messages) transfixed by a jack-knife into the very center of his wooden mantelpiece. Since working on our first case together a *Study in Scarlet* I discovered that he had a horror of destroying documents.

Thus month after month his papers accumulated, until every corner of the room was stacked with bundles of manuscripts which were on no account to be burned, and which could not be put away save by their owner.

What would appear to others as chaos, however, is to my friend a wealth of useful information. Throughout many cases, Holmes would dive into his apparent mess of random papers and artifacts, only to retrieve precisely the specific document or eclectic item he was looking for.

Without being under the watchful eye of Mrs. Hudson I also worried about Holmes health and how it was related to his particular eating habits. Unless insisted upon by Mrs. Hudson or if I was there to keep him company during the first meal of the day Holmes peculiar habits meant that he had no breakfast for himself.

It was one of his peculiarities that in his more intense moments he would permit himself no food, and I have known him to presume upon his iron strength until he has fainted from pure inanition.

Holmes rationalized this course of action with 'The faculties become refined when you starve them. Why, surely, as a doctor, my dear Watson, you must admit that what your digestion gains in the way of blood supply so much is lost to the brain.

I am a brain, Watson. The rest of me is a mere appendix. Therefore, it is the brain I must consider." Mrs. Hudson had always risen to the occasion. Her cuisine was a little limited, but she has as good an idea of breakfast as a Scotchwoman.

May 31: the first Zeppelin raid on London took place. The aerial raid kills 28 people and injures 60 more.

We said, "Look there it is! A long black cigar shaped object coming very slowly. I put my arms around my mother and I can tell you I don't know how we felt"....a young girl in London.

June 1915: The start of the second year of the war ... The second battle of Artois begins and will prove be the most important part of the Allied spring offensive of 1915.

This battle hopes to eventually capture Vimy Ridge, break through the German lines, and advance into the Douai plain. If successful, this action will cut key German railway lines and perhaps force them to retreat from their great salient bulging out into France.

July 13: Great Austro-German Offensive on Eastern front begins.

July 15: National Registration Act becomes law in Great Britain

Parliament (a Conservative coalition with a minority of the Liberals, under the leadership of Liberal David Lloyd George) passed the National Registration Act as a step towards stimulating recruitment and to discover how many men between the ages of 15 and 65 were engaged in each trade.

All those in this age range who were not already in the military were obliged to register, giving details of their employment details. The results of this census became available by mid-September 1915: it showed there were almost 5 million males of military age who were not in the forces, of which 1.6m were in the "starred" (protected, high skill) jobs. "

July 29: I received another sporadic letter from Holmes relating the life of a gentleman apiarist. Holmes seems (at least on the surface) to be settling in to a much simpler, less challenging and demanding way of life. As for me with the recent offensive my work has made more demands on my time. I give thanks for marrying a woman who knew that the life of a medical doctor is not an easy one.

It is comforting to know that when the motor taxi arrives at my home late in the evening that there are lights on downstairs and that supper is in the warming tray waiting for me and that unlike my friend Holmes it will be a shared meal.

But I fear that if this war goes on for too very much longer (there had been some talk of it being over by Christmas) that not only will all the combatants involved suffer in the end but so too will my marriage.

July 30: as the first Austrian shells fell on Belgrade, Russia, Serbia's Slav ally began to mobilize its men. The gradual slide into war now accelerated all over Europe.

An ever more frantic exchange of telegrams between cousins Kaiser Wilhelm of Germany and Tsar Nicholas of Russia did little to postpone the inevitable, for the war was now in the hands of the military. With Russian troops now on the move, Germany in turn began to mobilize its armies.

Tsar to Kaiser, July 29, 1:00 A.M.

Peter's Court Palais, 29 July

Sa Majesté l'Empereur
Neues Palais

Am glad you are back. In this serious moment, I appeal to you to help me. An ignoble war has been declared to a weak country. The indignation in Russia shared fully by me is enormous. I foresee that very soon I shall be overwhelmed by the pressure forced upon me and be forced to take extreme measures which will lead to war. To try and avoid such a calamity as a European war I beg you in the name of our old friendship to do what you can to stop your allies from going too far.

Nicky

28. July

It is with the gravest concern that I hear of the impression which the action of Austria against Serbia is creating in your country. The unscrupulous agitation that has been going on in Serbia for years has resulted in the outrageous crime, to which Archduke Francis Ferdinand fell a victim. The spirit that led Serbians to murder their own king and his wife still dominates the country.

You will doubtless agree with me that we both, you and me, have a common interest as well as all Sovereigns to insist that all the persons morally responsible for the dastardly murder should receive their deserved punishment. In this case politics plays no part at all.

On the other hand, I fully understand how difficult it is for you and your Government to face the drift of your public opinion. Therefore, with regard to the hearty and tender friendship which binds us both from long ago with firm ties,

I am exerting my utmost influence to induce the Austrians to deal straightly to arrive to a satisfactory understanding with you. I confidently hope that you will help me in my efforts to smooth over difficulties that may still arise.

Your very sincere and devoted friend and cousin

Willy

Kaiser to Tsar, July 29, 6:30 P.M.

Berlin, 29. July

I received your telegram and share your wish that peace should be maintained. But as I told you in my first telegram, I cannot consider Austria's action against Serbia an "ignoble" war. Austria knows by experience that Serbian promises ono paper are wholly unreliable. I understand its action must be judged as trending to get full guarantee that the Serbian promises shall become real facts. This my reasoning is borne out by the statement of the Austrian cabinet that Austria does not want to make any territorial conquests at the expense of Serbia.

I therefore suggest that it would be quite possible for Russia to remain a spectator of the Austro-Serbian conflict without involving Europe in the most horrible war she ever witnessed. I think a direct understanding between your Government and Vienna possible and desirable, and as I already telegraphed to you, my Government is continuing its exercises to promote it. Of course military measures on the part of Russia would be looked upon by Austria as a calamity we both wish to avoid and jeopardize my position as mediator which I readily accepted on your appeal to my friendship and my help.

Willy

Tsar to Kaiser, July 29, 8:20 P.M.

Peter's Court Palace, 29 July

Thanks for your telegram conciliatory and friendly. Whereas official message presented today by your ambassador to my minister was conveyed in a very different tone. Beg you to explain this divergency! It would be right to give over the Austro-Serbian problem to the Hague conference. Trust in your wisdom and friendship.

Your loving Nicky

46

Peter's Court Palais, 30 July

Thank you heartily for your quick answer. Am sending Tatischev this evening with instructions. The military measures which have now come into force were decided five days ago for reasons of defence on account of Austria's preparations. I hope from all my heart that these measures won't in any way interfere with your part as mediator which I greatly value. We need your strong pressure on Austria to come to an understanding with us.

Nicky

Berlin, 30. July

Best thanks for telegram. It is quite out of the question that my ambassador's language could have been in contradiction with the tenor of my telegram. Count Pourtalès was instructed to draw the attention of your government to the danger & grave consequences involved by a mobilisation; I said the same in my telegram to you. Austria has only mobilised against <u>Serbia</u> & only a <u>part</u> of her army. If, as it is now the case, according to the communication by you & your Government, Russia mobilises against Austria, my rôle as mediator you kindly intrusted me with, & which I accepted at you[r] express prayer, will be endangered if not ruined. The whole weight of the decision lies solely on you[r] shoulders now, who have to bear the responsibility for Peace or War.

Willy

Berlin, 31. July

On your appeal to my friendship and your call for assistance began to mediate between your and the Austro-Hungarian Government. While this action was proceeding your troops were mobilised against Austro-Hungary, my ally.

Thereby, as I have already pointed out to you, my mediation has been made almost illusory.

I have nevertheless continued my action. I now receive authentic news of serious preparations for war on my Eastern frontier. Responsibility for the safety of my empire forces preventive measures of defence upon me. In my endeavours to maintain the peace of the world I have gone to the utmost limit possible. The responsibility for the disaster which is now threatening the whole civilized world will not be laid at my door.

In this moment it still lies in your power to avert it. Nobody is threatening the honour or power of Russia who can well afford to await the result of my mediation.

My friendship for you and your empire, transmitted to me by my grandfather on his deathbed has always been sacred to me and I have honestly often backed up Russia when she was in serious trouble especially in her last war.

The peace of Europe may still be maintained by you, if Russia will agree to stop the milit. measures which must threaten Germany and Austro-Hungary.

Willy

Tsar to Kaiser, July 31
This and the previous telegram crossed.

Petersburg, Palace, 31 July

Sa Majesté l'Empereur, Neues Palais

I thank you heartily for your mediation which begins to give one hope that all may yet end peacefully. It is technically impossible to stop our military preparations which were obligatory owing to Austria's mobilisation. We are far from wishing war. As long as the negotiations with Austria on Serbia's account are taking place my troops shall not make any provocative action. I give you my solemn word for this. I put all my trust in Gods mercy and hope in your successful mediation in Vienna for the welfare of our countries and for the peace of Europe.

Your affectionate
Nicky

Peter's Court, Palace, 1 August

Sa Majesté l'Empereur
Berlin

*I received your telegram. Understand you are obliged to mobilise but wish to have the same guarantee from you as I gave you, that these measures **do not** mean war and that we shall continue negotiating for the benefit of our countries and universal peace deal to all our hearts.*

Our long proved friendship must succeed, with God's help, in avoiding bloodshed. Anxiously, full of confidence await your answer.

Nicky

Berlin, 1. August

Thanks for your telegram. I yesterday pointed out to your government the way by which alone war may be avoided. Although I requested an answer for noon today, no telegram from my ambassador conveying an answer from your Government has reached me as yet. I therefore have been obliged to mobilise my army.

Immediate affirmative clear and unmistakable answer from your government is the only way to avoid endless misery. Until I have received this answer alas, I am unable to discuss the subject of your telegram. As a matter of fact I must request you to immediately [sic] order your troops on no account to commit the slightest act of trespassing over our frontiers.

Willy

Wilhelm II or William II born 27 January 1859 was the last German Emperor (*Kaiser*) and King of Prussia, ruling the German Empire and the Kingdom of Prussia from 15 June 1888 to 9 November 1918.

He was a grandson of the British Queen Victoria and related to many monarchs and princes of Europe.

Crowned in 1888, he dismissed the Chancellor, Prince Otto von Bismarck, in 1890 and launched Germany on a bellicose "New Course" in foreign affairs that culminated in his support for Austria-Hungary in the crisis of July 1914 that led to World War I.

Nicholas II born1868 was the last Emperor of Russia, Grand Prince of Finland, and titular King of Poland. His official short title was Nicholas II, Emperor and Autocrat of All the Russias and he is known as Saint Nicholas the Passion-Bearer by the Russian Orthodox Church.

Nicholas II ruled from 1894 until his abdication on 15 March 1917. His reign saw Imperial Russia go from being one of the foremost great powers of the world to economic and military collapse. Critics nicknamed him Bloody Nicholas because of the Khodynka Tragedy, Bloody Sunday, the anti-Semitic pogroms, his execution of political opponents, and his pursuit of military campaigns on a hitherto unprecedented scale.

During his rule, Russia was defeated in the Russo-Japanese War, including the almost total annihilation of the Russian fleet at the Battle of Tsushima. As head of state, he approved the Russian mobilization of August 1914, which marked the beginning of Russia's involvement in World War I, a war in which 3.3 million Russians were killed.

The Imperial Army's big losses and the monarchy's incompetent handling with the war, along with other policies directed by Nicholas during his reign, are often cited as the leading causes of the fall of the Romanov dynasty.

...many could not even load their rifles and as for their shooting the less said the better. Such people could not really be considered soldiers at all...a Russian field commander.

August 12 British inventors begin work on what will become the world's first tracked armored vehicle. Nicknamed "Little Willie" it makes its debut on September 8. Suggestions by Winston Churchill on December 24 that the secret weapon should be described as a water tank is accepted and the term "tank" enters the common language.

September 25: Allied Autumn Offensive begins: - Battle of Loos begins. Third Battle of Artois begins. Second Battle of Champagne begins

October 1: It was with some sadness that I had to sign yet another death certificate late last night for one of the many severely wounded soldiers on the wards here in the hospital. He had passed away from injuries received as a result of enemy shrapnel.

Among his few personal effects on the night table next to the bed was a well worn dark brown leather covered book. I had picked it up to look at it merely out of curiosity, not intending to open it and observe the personal contents it held.

I started to place it back where I found it when a young male voice in the bed next to the one that was now empty said "go ahead sir, I don' t think Stanley would mind you reading his diary."

Feeling for a moment as if I was about to eavesdrop on a private conversation I hesitated then realizing I would never be able to experience this war first hand I thought by reading a bit of this record of a soldier's daily life I might get to know a little about conditions at the front. I randomly opened the chronicle I was holding in my hand to a page and started to read two brief entries.

Thursday:

We fell in two deep and at the slope to hear a Court Martial Sentence read out, this morning. The prisoner, an Australian was escorted by two sentries and he was charged with having been drunk on sentry duty and having stolen two tins of condensed milk from Government Stores.

The Assistant Provost Marshal read the charge first and then the sentence. He was sentenced to 3 years penal servitude. The prisoner flinched at that. Reading on the A.P.M. said that the sentence was commuted to 3 months field punishment. The man was so dazed that he had to ask afterwards what he got. One silly fool told him 3 years and 3 months. The shock of hearing himself sentenced to three years stunned him and he failed to hear the rest.

Saturday:

I received a much appreciated and anticipated letter from my special girl Virginia during a lull in the fighting this afternoon. She tells me that she and the other sisters feel as if their shifts will never come to an end with the number of injured soldiers that arrive at the hospital each day. In spite of the fact that most of the doctors seem to have little regard or respect for the important role in care the sisters provide ...there is a Doctor Watson Virginia speaks highly of.

After I had finished reading the entries and returned the soldiers diary to where I had originally found it I started to think that maybe I should turn my hand to leaving a legacy of Holmes cases. Although I was the biographer (his Boswell) of only 17 of his 23 solved cases I believed that a published and bound collection would be of interest to any one who had faithfully followed my articles in the Strand over the years.

Hopefully I thought that despite the fact my friend was not living in the city he would still accept Mary's and my invitation for Christmas day. It would be at that time I would propose the venture.

October 15: Austria-Hungary invades the Kingdom of Serbia. Kingdom of Bulgaria enters the war, invading Kingdom of Serbia. The retreat of the Serbian First Army towards Greece begins the Serbian Campaign.

November 12: Sykes-Picot Agreement: The governments of Britain and France secretly agree to overtake the Middle-Eastern regions of the Ottoman Empire, and establish their own zones of influence.

December 20: I received a telegram from Holmes after dinner confirming his arrival at King Cross Station on December 25 at 1:00 p.m. and that he would arrange to take a motor taxi from the station to be at our house for 2:00 p.m.

Chapter 5

December 25. After Holmes had entered our home he closed the front door to keep out the late afternoon winter conditions. He removed his snow covered top hat, coat and foot wear, then like a magician he produced a very familiar pair of brown bedroom slippers put them on and bearing a Christmas gift under his left arm followed Mary and me into the parlor.

While Holmes and Mary enjoyed the smells of the Christmas tree, dinner being cooked and chatted I lit the candles on the tree then stepped back for all to appreciate "It gladdens my heart to see this little bit of brightness at such a dark time of year" my friend stated as he pointed towards the universal secular symbol of the season.

All three of us in the room understood what was being said...dark not only because the sun set so early at this time of year, but also because a kind of darkness had settled over most of Europe.

Then realizing he was still holding onto his Christmas present to us Holmes stated in mock surprise to break the somber moment "Ah a gift from myself, and my very industrious bees to you both" at which time he handed a very simply but elegantly wrapped present to Mary.

"John, Sherlock's present is there on the mantle." I went and retrieved his gift which we both hoped would be a much used and appreciated present.

Now that Holmes had become a confirmed gentleman bee keeper and knowing his unending thirst for knowledge when I had on one of my rare free Saturdays in early December gone to Cecil Court to do some Christmas shopping and paid a visit to Watkins books to inquire what practical tomes on bee keeping they had in their collection.

The two books I finally selected, purchased and had gift wrapped were a first edition yellow cloth bound copy of "Honey Production in the British Isles" written by R.O.B Manley and a second edition blue cloth bound copy of "Practical Queen-Rearing" written by Frank Pellett. This was our present to him.

Handing him the package with my left hand I then extended my right hand and wished Holmes a Merry Christmas.

"A very Merry Christmas to you Watson" seasonally returned Holmes as he heartily shook my hand…then in a very rare display of tenderness Holmes turned to Mary gently took hold of both of her hands in his and wished her a Merry Christmas…"and a very Merry Christmas to you too Sherlock" was her warm smiling return.

Then we all sat down to open presents before beginning the Christmas meal. Holmes was surprised and genuinely pleased with his two new books.

They would I had no doubt be added to his growing library on all things concerning bees. We in turn were surprised when we opened our present from Holmes and found it contained four medium sized sealed glass pickling jars full of golden yellow honey.

Despite it being the second year of the war (there was now some war rationing at home) our Christmas day meal together was the same as it had been in previous years. There was roast goose (a tradition started with the case of the Blue Carbuncle) Brussels sprouts, roast potatoes, cranberry sauce, rich nutty stuffing and lashings of hot gravy.

Christmas at the front however was celebrated much differently... life in the trenches was abominable. Continuous sniping, machinegun fire and artillery shelling took a deadly toll. The misery was heightened by the ravages of Mother Nature, including rain, snow and cold. Many of the trenches, especially those in the low-lying British sector to the west, were continually flooded, exposing the troops to frost bite and "trench foot."

Trench foot is a medical condition caused by prolonged exposure of the feet to damp, unsanitary, and cold conditions. It is one of many immersion foot syndromes. The use of the word "trench" in the name of this condition is a reference to trench warfare, mainly associated with World War I.

Trench foot occurs when feet are cold and damp while wearing constricting footwear. Unlike frostbite, trench foot does not require freezing temperatures and can occur in temperatures up to 60° Fahrenheit The condition can occur with as little as thirteen hours' exposure. The mechanism of tissue damage is not fully understood. Excessive sweating or hyperhidrosis has long been regarded as a contributory cause.

This treacherous monotony was briefly interrupted during an unofficial and spontaneous "Christmas Truce" that began on Christmas Eve. Both sides had received Christmas packages of food and presents. The clear skies that ended the rain further lifted the spirits on both sides of no-mans-land.

This was a much appreciated change in the usual diet of a soldier. British Daily Ration, 1 1/4 lb. fresh or frozen meat, or 1 lb. preserved or salt meat; 1 1/4 lb. bread, or 1 lb. biscuit or flour; 4 oz. bacon; 3 oz. cheese; 5/8 oz. tea; 4 oz. jam; 3 oz. sugar; 1/2 oz. salt; 1/36 oz. pepper; 1/20 oz. mustard; 8 oz. fresh or 2 oz. dried vegetables; 1/10 gill lime juice if fresh vegetables not issued;* 1/2 gill rum;* not exceeding 2 oz. tobacco per week at discretion of commanding officer

German Daily Ration, 26 1/2 oz. bread, or 17 1/2 oz. field biscuit, or 14 oz. egg biscuit; 13 oz. fresh or frozen meat, or 7 oz. preserved meat; 53 oz. potatoes, or 4 1/2-9 oz. vegetables, or 2 oz. dried vegetables, or 21 oz. mixed potatoes and dried vegetables; 9/10 oz. coffee, or 1/10 oz. tea; 7/10 oz. sugar; 9/10 oz. salt; two cigars and two cigarettes or 1 oz. pipe tobacco, or 9/10 oz. plug tobacco, or 1/5 oz. snuff; at discretion of commanding officer

The Germans seem to have made the first move. During the evening of December 24 they delivered a chocolate cake to the British line accompanied by a note that proposed a cease fire so that the Germans could have a concert.

The British accepted the proposal and offered some tobacco as their present to the Germans. The good will soon spread along the length of the British line. Enemy soldiers shouted to one another from the trenches, joined in singing songs and soon met one another in the middle of no-mans-land to talk, exchange gifts and in some areas to take part in impromptu soccer matches.

After a sumptuous festive meal Mary dismissed both Holmes and myself to the parlor and told us that she would join both us after she had dealt with the remains of the meal and the dishes they had been served on.

Now standing near the hearth for warmth and not sure where to place my first step with what I was about to ask I blindly started in "Holmes I have an idea I would like you to consider." "What is it Watson?" he questioned while he struck a match on the brick face of the hearth to light his pipe.

Having not been rejected I went on a little more confidently "Back in October I happened upon a young soldiers diary, unfortunately he had succumbed to his wounds…the contents I read were of no real importance but reading it gave me the idea of publishing a bound collection of the cases I have documented for you…an anthology or memoir as it were."

Before we all knew it our time together was at an end. As if to signal this Holmes reached into his vest pocket for his pocket watch to check the time then purposely made his way from the parlor to the front entrance to collect and put on all of his winter outerwear.

Mary, while wiping her hands dry on a dish towel was making her way from the pantry back to the parlor spotted Holmes in the entrance starting to put on his coat and reacting to his departure inquired "So soon Sherlock?"

As he was getting ready to leave Mary (now by my side) and I, not sure about Holmes immediate plans offered to let him stay with us for the night so that he could catch his train back to Doncaster early on Boxing Day morning.

Doing up the top buttons of his coat then donning his top hat Holmes replied "I thank you Watson and your wife for your wonderful festive hospitality and Christmas gift, but I have imposed on you both for too long. Besides I think I see my hired transport that will take me back to the city is now arriving in front of your home."

Knowing that Holmes was a man of meticulous detail and never left anything to chance I was not surprised when I saw through the falling snow the predicted motor taxi and driver now waiting in the lane.

Still a little bit concerned about my friend and that it was dark and had started to snow again I asked if he was going to wait overnight at the Kings Cross Station for his morning train.

To assure me he answered "No I have arranged to spend the night with my brother Mycroft at his club...thereby guaranteeing I will arrive in plenty of time tomorrow morning to board my train home."

So with a final round of hearty (for me) and tender (for Mary) "Merry Christmases" Holmes, now well bundled up made his way (with his present) back down the snow covered path and entered his waiting hired transport.

Chapter 6

1916...

"Not a tree stands. Not a square foot of surface has escaped mutilation. There is nothing but mud and gaping shell holes; a chaotic wilderness of violently created craters, rim overlapping rim; and, in the bottom of many, the bodies of the dead"...a British soldier at the front.

... ...

A bitter winter returned again to the much fought over battlefield...the soft cottony snow of January began to slowly and gently swirl downward from a bleakly lit lead grey sky... its act of falling was as if it was trying to desperately heal a deserted, scarred, silent and utterly desolate landscape... individual descending flakes...each one in their turn creating a cold white shroud to respectfully conceal the dead of each countries army.

Now every anonymous unmoving and silent soldier having done his duty found himself haphazardly congregated next to other nameless still and silent soldiers in no mans land...all are at rest and are now past feelings of animosity and hatred towards the others who have fallen there.

Brave men...foolish men who because of continuous sniping, withering machinegun fire and artillery shelling can never be returned to where they had first recklessly embarked from for King and Kaiser. They had not been given a proper burial and had not been able to make the final few moments of their life on this earth peaceful. They did not die in the company of their brothers in arms; in the end they died alone and unknown.

....

"The turmoil of our feelings was called forth by rage, alcohol and thirst for blood as we stepped out, heavily yet irresistibly, for the enemy's lines"...a German soldier at the front

January 13 The Battle of Wadi occurs between Allied British and Ottoman Empire forces, during the Mesopotamian campaign.

January 29 Paris is bombed by German zeppelins for the first time

The New Year settled back into a familiar routine...the fighting in Europe picked up from where it had stopped during the Christmas truce. I was back to carrying out my role of a medical doctor trying to save lives and offer some peace and comfort to the dying...and with what little spare time I had to be a good and attentive husband and home owner.

The only concern I carried over from 1915 to 1916 was Holmes somewhat cryptic and almost careless reply on Christmas night to my request of creating the anthology of his successfully solved cases that I had recorded and documented for him.

His answer as he was getting ready to leave by motor taxi to be taken to the Diogenes club (his brother Mycroft's club) came about as a result of the first published (in the Strand Magazine) Holmes story, A Study in Scarlet.

From the first I was very impressed by Holmes's elegant handling of the case and was so incensed by Scotland Yard's claiming full credit for its solution that I exclaimed: "Your merits should be publicly recognized." Holmes had observed "Out of my last fifty-three cases, my name has only appeared in four, and the police have had all the credit in forty-nine."

To let his skills as a detective be known to the public I noted "You should publish an account of the case. If you won't, I will for you." Holmes suavely responded to my unbounded enthusiasm with:

"You may do what you like, Doctor." Hence I did write the story and presented it as "a reprint from the reminiscences of John H. Watson". I knew the wellspring of his attitude was the Sign of Four, my second documented case.

Holmes commented on my first effort as a biographer…professionally (no doubt) but with a distinct lack of enthusiasm: "I glanced over it" he started. "Honestly, I cannot congratulate you upon it.

"Detection is, or ought to be, an exact science and should be treated in the same cold and unemotional manner. You have attempted to tinge it with romanticism"… (If there had been a place and time for Holmes to cringe this would have been the place and the time).

"The only point in the case which deserved any mention was the curious analytical reasoning from effects to causes, by which I succeeded in unraveling it."

In some later stories, Holmes criticizes me for my writings, usually because I relate them as exciting stories rather than as objective and detailed reports focusing on what Holmes regards as the pure "science" of his craft.

In spite of the outwardly cold reception I often received whenever Holmes happened to notice my entering notes in my journal I think a small part of him, secretly enjoyed the admiration and fame he was receiving from the readers of the Strand Magazine.

These were genuinely interested people who avidly followed his exploits month by month through my well documented cases. Because of newspaper articles and my stories, Holmes became well known as a detective, and many clients ask for his help instead of (or alongside) the police.

For the reader not familiar with the publication I made notice of ... The Strand Magazine is a monthly magazine composed of fictional stories and factual articles founded by George Newnes. It was first published in the United Kingdom in January 1891.

Despite the fact that Holmes, by default had left the project in my hands to either start or dismiss I would not think it proper to choose any course of action until I had a clear answer from him as to which direction to proceed.

January 16 War Office takes over anti-aircraft defense of London from the Admiralty, and becomes responsible for anti-aircraft defense generally throughout the country.

"A glorious death! Fight on and fly on to the last drop of blood and the last drop of petrol... a death for a knight"... a pilot in the Imperial German Army Air Service (Luftstreitkräfte).

"There are certain instances whereby pilots would arrive in the morning as replacements and be dead by the afternoon and hadn't even unpacked their kit"... a British Royal Flying Corps pilot

World War I was the first war in which aircraft were deployed on a large scale. Tethered observation balloons had already been employed in several wars, and would be used extensively for artillery spotting. Germany employed Zeppelins for reconnaissance over the North Sea and strategic bombing raids over England.

Airplanes were just coming into military use at the outset of the war. Initially, they were used mostly for reconnaissance. Pilots and engineers learned from experience, leading to the development of many specialized types, including fighters, bombers, and ground-attack airplanes.

Ace fighter pilots were portrayed as modern knights, and many became popular heroes. The war also saw the appointment of high-ranking officers to direct the belligerent nations' air war effort. While the impact of aircraft on the course of war was limited, many of the lessons learned would be applied in future wars.

When Europe went to war in 1914, the heavier than air flying machine had only become fact just a few years previously. Armies and navies, however quickly realized that the air craft could be used as a means of reconnaissance and could possibly fulfill other roles as well.

The aircraft that went to war were of three basic types: monoplane and biplane tractor aircraft, with the engine in the nose; and biplane pushers, with the engine mounted in the rear.

Trench life had its own routine with bombardments by day and trench mending, patrols, delivery of supplies and new troops at night. This was siege warfare with modern weaponry adapted and invented to inflict maximum damage. Little territory changed hands. But by 1916 both Allied and the German High Command came up with plans to break the dead lock.

Often after days of ruthless killing and sweltering heat, the stench from no mans' land would become unbearable for the inhabitants of both sets of trenches, often no more than twenty yards apart. A general call would go out for men from both sides to collect and bury their dead during a brief cease fire.

"What was a man's life in this wilderness whose vapor was laden with the reek of thousands upon thousands of decaying bodies? At this place chivalry took a final farewell"...a Canadian soldier at the front.

The new French Anglo was to coordinate a strategy which would pull the German armies in different directions. Offenses were to start as near simultaneously as possible on several fronts.

While Russian and Italian armies engaged the Central Powers in renewed fighting on the eastern and Isonzo Fronts French troops with the support of the British were to launch an attack on the Germans at the Somme in July.

The Battle of the Somme (French: *Bataille de la Somme*, German: *Sommeschlacht*), also known as the Somme Offensive, took place between 1 July and 18 November 1916 in the Somme department, on either side of the river Somme.

The battle consisted of an offensive by the British and French armies against the German Army, which, since invading France in August 1914, had occupied large areas of the country.

The Battle of the Somme was one of the largest battles of the war; by the time fighting paused in late autumn 1916 the forces involved had suffered more than 1 million casualties, making it one of the bloodiest military operations ever recorded.

But as soon as the date for the Anglo French offensive had been agreed, the German commander in Chief, Erich von Falkenhayn, stole the initiative from the Allies with his plan to break the dead lock.

On February 21 a massive German bombardment launched an offensive on a small sector of the front line near the fortress town of Verdun, a place of great psychological significance to the French and a symbol of the Franco Prussian War. (19 July 1870 – 10 May 1871), after an initial advance, and six days of fighting, the Germans were halted.

The casualties were very high on both sides. The French were ordered to hold out and defend Verdun at all costs. By May the fighting was still intense.

February 21 The German High Command launches an offensive (codename "*Gericht*, Judgment"). The battle began at 07:15 on this day with a 10-hour artillery bombardment by 808 guns. The Germans fire close to 1,000,000 shells along a front about 19 miles long by 3.1 miles wide. The highest concentration of that fire is aimed at the French positions situated on the right (east) bank of the Meuse river. This action would come to be known as the Battle of Verdun.

Chapter 7

March 1 Airplane raid on Broadstairs and Margate, one killed.

After the Snow Drops, Daffodils and Crocuses started to appear from dormant dark earth flower beds in the public parks around London and in the flower beds in front of our house the new arrivals brought some much needed variety of color and vibrancy to what was otherwise a very drab and somber world.

In 1915, the western Allies sent a massive invasion force of British, Indian, Australian, and New Zealand troops to attempt to open up the strait. During the Gallipoli campaign, Turkish troops trapped the Allies on the beaches of the Gallipoli peninsula. The campaign results did damage the career of Sir Winston Churchill, then the First Lord of the Admiralty, who eagerly promoted the use of Royal Navy sea power to force open the straits.

The straits were mined by the Turks to prevent Allied ships from penetrating them, but in minor actions, two submarines, one British and one Australian, did succeed in penetrating the minefields.

The British one sank an obsolete Turkish pre-dreadnought battleship off the Golden Horn of Istanbul. Sir Ian Hamilton's Mediterranean Expeditionary Force was unsuccessful in its attempt to capture the Gallipoli peninsula, and its withdrawal was ordered in January 1916, after 10 months fighting and more than 200,000 casualties.

March 18 A British attack on the Dardanelles fails.

March 24 The SS *Sussex* is torpedoed by SM *UB-29* on a voyage from Folkestone to Dieppe. This action results in the drafting of the Sussex pledge. The document is drawn up to avoid any armed conflicts with America.

Germany pledges that passenger ships will not be targeted; merchant ships will not be sunk until the presence of weapons had been established, if necessary by a search of the ship. In addition, merchant ships will not be sunk without provision for the safety of passengers and crew.

It is here in my narrative that I bring the readers attention to the details of a number of "chance" meetings that took place in early March in Switzerland between two very different and unlikely people.

I say chance somewhat skeptically because Holmes and I could never really be certain if in fact the meetings were a result of a purely set of random events, some might say serendipity or had they been carefully planned by one individual and one foreign government to happen where and when they did.

The encounters took place between a young assistant patent clerk named Albert Einstein and a young famed exotic dancer who was touring Europe at the time. This meeting took place at the large outdoor patio which adjoined the Café Odeon in Zurich.

The Café, located at Limmatqui 2 is the noted social hub of the city. It is active with famished customers from early morning until late afternoon. The Odeon had built its impeccable reputation on its extensive menu, service and the attractive alfresco patio décor, which included green wrought iron tables with matching chairs and large tan colored parasols that provided cooling shade to the diners during the hottest and brightest part of the day.

Any one choosing (including The Dadaists, Trotsky, Lenin and any literary figures) to have an early lunch or late afternoon refreshment had an excellent choice between Swiss and European cuisine as well as an impressive selection of wines that would easily compliment any meal eaten there.

The attentive professional waiters who worked themselves gracefully and skillfully among the packed tables taking food and drink orders and delivering the anticipated nourishment and refreshments to waiting patrons had a reputation that went well beyond the Cafe and the city of Zurich.

The young assistant patent clerk, Albert Einstein, was born in Ulm, in the Kingdom of Württemberg in the German Empire on 14 March 1879 and was employed at the Federal Office for Intellectual Property, a patent office in Bern in 1903.

He was an assistant examiner and as mentioned the young famed exotic dancer was touring Europe at the time. It is of some interest to note that much of Einstein's work at the patent office related to a later change of career and that he would go on to become a noted researcher in the new field of physics

The mentioned young ladies name before the start of her famous career had been Margaretha Geertruida "M'greet" Zelle who was born in the Dutch East Indies. She claimed that she had been born in India, and she was also said to be Javanese, Eurasian, or even Jewish. In Javanese (Indonesian), "Mata Hari" means "Eye of Dawn," or early sunrise.

"Mata Hari" is also one of the many names of Parvati, a Hindu goddess and consort of Shiva, the god of creation, destruction, and dance. In fact, Margaretha Zelle had no Asian blood at all. She was born in Leeuwarden, the capital of the Dutch province of Friesland. Her father, Adam Zelle, was a prosperous hatter of German descent. Her mother, Antje Van Der Meulen, came from a well-off Frisian family.

It was in 1905 that she began to win fame as an exotic dancer and adopted the stage name *Mata Hari*. She was a contemporary of dancers Isadora Duncan and Ruth St. Denis, leaders in the early modern dance movement, which around the turn of the 20th century looked to Asia and Egypt for artistic inspiration. She posed as a Java princess of priestly Hindu birth, pretending to have been immersed in the art of sacred Indian dance since childhood.

Mata Hari always maintained that her dances were authentically Asian and had religious significance, just as she also claimed to be Indian or Indonesian herself. Ignorance of Asian dance was so widespread at the time that few challenged her claims.

Though taken seriously both by critics and a few anthropologists, Mata Hari's dances were in fact a pastiche of her own invention. Her success was largely due to the contemporary fascinations with exotic eroticism and all things Oriental.

Later Margaretha's stage name and her other real or imagined career would take on more significance for everyone she had come into contact with. It would be the chief cause as to whether Holmes would permanently come out of retirement and again take up the reins of a consulting detective or go back to the solitary company of his bees.

Chapter 8

April 20 Disguised German transport "Aud" sinks herself after capture while trying to land arms on Irish coast

April 24 – April 30 the Easter uprising occurs in Ireland

April 26 Organized at a time when the British Empire is heavily engaged in the First World War. It would be the most significant uprising in Ireland's history since the rebellion of 1798. The rising is mounted by Irish republicans with the aim of ending British rule in Ireland and establishing the Irish Republic.

The Rising would last from Easter Monday 24 April to 30 April 1916. Members of the Irish Volunteers—led by schoolteacher and barrister Pádraig (Patrick) Pearse, joined by the smaller Irish Citizen Army of James Connolly, along with 200 members of Cumann na mBan—seize key locations in Dublin and proclaim the Irish Republic independent of Britain.

The Rising would in the end be suppressed after seven days of fighting, and its leaders would be court-martialled and executed, but it succeeded in bringing physical force republicanism back to the forefront of Irish politics.

The newspapers in Dublin and Belfast at the time denounced the Easter Rising. The Irish Independent - owned by the Dublin entrepreneur William Martin Murphy - called for the execution of the rebel leaders and in particular James Connolly who had organized a strike against Murphy's Dublin Tramway Company in 1913. A few days after the Rising the then pro-Union Irish Times put out an emergency edition and urged its readers to stay at home and read Shakespeare until events calmed down.

April 27 I was attending to one of my patients during my morning rounds at St. Bartholomew's when a nursing sister whose name I believe was Virginia Powell approached and informed me that I had a visitor waiting in the main reception area of the hospital who asked to meet with me.

Not knowing anyone who would come to meet with me during my work day I was curious about the visitor. "Did he give a name Sister?" I asked as I was removing my stethoscope from my patients' chest and instructing him to button his pajama top.

"Einstein…Dr. Watson and he knows of you and Mr. Holmes." The name not registering I queried "Is there anything else you can tell me about him" curious to know more about my caller.

She concentrated for a moment then replied hopefully "He has what sounds to be a German accent." Considering the present situation I had cause for concern thinking that the individual might be some type of German spy in search of military information therefore I decided to be cautious and instruct the nursing sister to tell the gentleman I was already engaged.

But because this person had knowledge of Holmes and me curiosity won out and German or not, I decided to meet my morning visitor briefly. That way I could discover why he had sought me out. "Thank you sister, I will meet with Mr. Einstein briefly" I said as I made my way to greet my mystery caller.

The walk down the main hallway from the ward to my destination presented a barometer of how the war had been going. Where there had once been hospital beds in their proper orderly location, now each of the wards I passed was now crowded with beds.

Because of the volume of wounded we were now treating the halls or passage ways from each ward had also become temporary (albeit permanent) hospital wards. As you walked past the wards the patients in them were only case numbers and abstracts until you had to treat them.

Then war wounded in these make shift wards became very real and you couldn't help but feel their pain and see their suffering

April 27 Battle of Hulluch: The 47th Brigade, 16th Irish Division is decimated in one of the most heavily concentrated German gas attacks of the war.

My visitor's accent turned out in fact to be Swiss and not German. Albert Einstein as he formally introduced himself was an assistant examiner employed at the Federal Office for Intellectual Property, a patent office in Bern, Switzerland

His some what short stature, rumpled appearance and dress was what one would expect of a person who sits behind a desk all day examining patent applications and either stamping their approval to be filed or rejecting them to be returned to their applicant.

When I inquired about the somewhat slow pace of his position the assistant examiner smiled and replied "It gives me a lot of time to think and conduct what I like to think of as thought experiments Dr. Watson."

After exchanging formal pleasantries including the fact that Einstein had been faithfully following my chronicles of Holmes cases in the Berner Zeitung (a Bern Swiss newspaper). He then asked if there was somewhere we could go to have some privacy and talk.

As we were standing close to the main entrance of the hospital it meant a lot of people milling around, coming and going and definitely offered no privacy. I knew that the hospital library was probably not in use at this time of day and being a short distance from where we were I suggested we continue our conversation there.

I closed the double doors and engaged the lock indicating that until someone was in dire need of a medical text what was shared between Einstein and I would go no further. With the sound of the assuring "click" of the door locking he began. "Dr. Watson, I have come to seek both your and Mr. Holmes help in retrieving something that may have accidently been given away and that I wish to have returned to me.

Chapter 9

The thing Einstein had given away (as he put it) and now wanted found and returned was not anything tangible that could be experienced by any of a persons five senses. It was in fact only an idea, theory or concept, that he was concerned could fall into the wrong hands and radically alter the outcome of the war.

Wanting to fully explain the idea, in terms I could relate too and understand was frustrating because of the limited time we had before I had to return to my patients. "I'm in London for a few more days and I have a room at the Oxford Hotel near Kensington Gardens.'

"Perhaps, you, Mr. Holmes and I could arrange to meet there later and without any time restrictions I could impress upon you both how important it is that I get this item back." While checking my pocket watch to see how much time I had left before returning to my rounds I explained Holmes present status but assured Einstein that I had the necessary skills to do any preliminary investigation work ahead of time before requesting Holmes take time away from his bees and join me. Then as much to bolster my confidence as Einstein's I stated "I have not lived for years with Sherlock Holmes and studied his methods for nothing."

Starting to detect the sensitive nature of what was about to be revealed I suggested that instead of meeting in public at the hotel...a meeting of this nature would be better suited to happen during a private dinner at 126 Hill House Road.

After making the arrangements for later and as I was walking Einstein back to the front entrance of the hospital I casually asked who this information had accidentally been given to. Einstein for a moment had a look of wistfulness and nostalgia then answered "As always to a beautiful young lady."

Later that evening at our home during dinner...

"Some more roast beef Mr. Einstein?" Mary asked as she lifted the serving platter in the direction of our guest. "No thank you Mrs. Watson, but if you have some blueberries they will serve to demonstrate and explain to you both the theory I started telling your husband about this morning."

Mary got up from the dinner table and returned carrying a small white porcelain bowl almost filled to the edge with small blue and purple orbs. She placed the bowl on the table in front of Einstein "more than enough thank you Mrs. Watson."

Our guest reflectively looked at the bowl and its contents for a few minutes, and then as if starting a university lecture he asked both of us (as if we were his students) "How do we conventionally extract energy from a raw source?" Mary and I of course realized that this was only a rhetorical question and waited for our guest to continue.

By burning coal or wood, compressing petrol in a cylinder then igniting it much as a motor car does, lighting a candle or gas lamp." The only problem with this is that it is inefficient you never get the full potential of energy from the raw material being utilized."

"But I have developed a theory that would allow you to achieve a very large amount of energy from a very small source. The source is mineral called uranium…which in your medical practice you may already have some knowledge of Dr. Watson."

I admitted that I had heard of the material but my knowledge consisted of only knowing that if was handled for too long a person would develop what was known as radiation poisoning and eventually die.

Removing one particular blueberry from the rest Einstein held it between his thumb and first finger of his right hand. "Let us say that this blueberry represents a small amount of uranium." Here Einstein paused while Mary and I mentally transformed the harmless piece of fruit into something more lethal.

"Now conventional wisdom would say that we can't by any means release the potential energy stored inside." Seeing my skeptical reaction that something so small could contain any form of energy Einstein assured me that there was more energy inside than could be imagined.

"With my theory Dr. and Mrs. Watson a process I have called nuclear fusion, which simply translated, means that when a lot of pressure is equally applied to say this blueberry watch what happens."

It was at this point our guest slowly brought his thumb and fore finger together, we watched as the small blue berry went from being round to squat to bursting open thereby releasing the juice and seeds that had been stored inside.

Then while wiping his right hand clean he solemnly stated "Instead of dealing with the contents of a small piece of fruit imagine instead dealing with the contents of uranium. You would have an explosive force of unimaginable power and life destroying devastation. Mary turned to me, grasped both my hands and with a look of potential fear upon her face said "John, you must contact Sherlock straight away."

Leaving the dinner table and making our way to the parlor I tried to get a full grasp of the problem I had been presented and using, as Holmes would observe, my limited detective skills I went in search of the rest of the clues.

When we were all comfortably seated and I had attended to the coal fire in the hearth I questioned our guest as delicately as I could as to who the young lady was that he had mentioned in the hospital library.

"Her name is Margaretha Geertruida "M'greet" Zelle, Doctor Watson and she told me during our first meeting at an outdoor patio in Zurich that she is a dancer and an entertainer."

Hearing of the lady's profession gave me more cause for concern. From previous cases I had shared with Holmes I had discovered that such persons tend to lead double lives. A two faceted life as it were, a public and innocent one on the surface masking or hiding a more sinister and devious one.

As if to confirm this suspicion Einstein continued "I must admit I had shared the occasional glance and admired her at the outdoor patio without being forward enough to go to her table and introduce myself".

"It was after a number of furtive shared experiences that Margaretha took the initiative to come and introduce her to me. It was interesting Dr. Watson that after formal introductions were made and she sat down and shared my table with me it was if I had already known the lady for some time."

"It must have been the right combination or the time of day, the food I had ordered, my choice of wine, her pleasant and warm company that made me divulge as much as I did about my life. My tedious occupation and how I spent my time in thought experiments concerning my theories about nuclear fusion."

"How many occasions did you meet with her?" "Enough times Dr. Watson to think that I might have a standing engagement and have something pleasant to look forward to each lunch time." "But I remember our last lunch together when I asked Margaretha if I could expect her company tomorrow when she calmly announced that she was leaving Switzerland to go back on tour."

"She assured me that she would stay in touch by letters and telegrams to let me know where she was performing and when she would return to Zurich. Which of course she didn't and this is one of the many reasons I have sought yours and Mr. Holmes help."

Chapter 10

April 27. Martial law proclaimed in Dublin and the county as a result of events occurring on April 24

April 28. Now with a growing sense of urgency I made a stop the next morning at the Electrical and International Company (a telegraph office) formed in 1855 located at 314 Oxford Street to send a cable to Holmes requesting his expedient return to London before continuing on to the hospital to start my day.

Within the company's imposed 20 word, 2 shilling limits I tried my best to sum up the contents of the two meetings with the Swiss patent clerk and give Holmes some measure as to the gravity of the situation.

I found myself using this form of communication because my friend had stated in one of his sporadic letters to me that one of the amenities that he had found attractive about the "Beeches" was that it lacked the constant and irritating annoyance (as he put it) of a constantly ringing telephone.

I dictated the contents of the telegram to the clerk who would then send it to the General Post Office in Doncaster. It read as follows…matter of gravest concern (stop) return to London a.s.a.p. (stop) have information that could potentially change outcome of the war (stop) Watson (stop).

Knowing that the dispatch would be sent and received almost instantly by the telegraph lines strung between the two cities I could bear a short unavoidable delay knowing that my important message would have to be first written out when received and then delivered in person to Holmes. Of course the individual carrying out this task would have to wait for his reply.

I left instructions with the telegraph agency as to where I could be contacted at St. Bartholomew's or at my residence when Holmes reply would eventually be directed back to me. There was some small amount of anxiety when I left the building not being sure as to when I would receive a reply and where I would receive it.

By the end of my day of hospital rounds, of seeing patients, filling out forms and prescriptions I had not received the much awaited for reply. On the journey home that evening I had to assure myself that as I walked through the front door of my home Mary would hand me the much anticipated envelope.

April 29 – 30 having yet to obtain a reply I began to formulate the reasons for its absence. Although highly unlikely it was a remote possibility that there had been a break in the telegraph wires between London and Doncaster and my message had not been received or that the return message had not been collected.

The other more likely possibility was the fact that because of the war Holmes now wanted to distance and isolate himself as much as he could from present events. The message in all probability had been received and the courier informed to come back at a later time for a reply. At which point this new urgent communication now joined the many others of his unanswered correspondences filed in Holmes unique manner.

Chapter 11

May 1. Collapse of Irish Rebellion – all the leaders involved surrender.

May 3. German airship "L.-20" returning from raid on Scotland is wrecked at Stavanger (Norway). Three Irish rebel leaders executed

May 4 and as I am not sure how unsafe the material Fraulein Zelle had acquired from Einstein during their afternoon visits in Zurich and more importantly what she intended to do with the sensitive facts made me change my week end plans. Instead of spending two peaceful days away from the war driven turmoil of St Bartholomew's I, with my wife's very understanding blessing, was now standing on the busy passenger platform with a bag in hand at Kings Cross Station waiting for the 4:15 p.m. "The East Midlands Express" a Great Northern Railroad passenger train.

I would have about two hours traveling time going north from London to Doncaster. This would give me ample time to formulate one of many plausible reasons as to why Holmes should place the care of his beloved bees and cottage to a close neighbor and return with me. Yet, I would need his help in retrieving something that may have been accidently given away by Einstein that he now wished to have returned.

While listening to the carriages steel wheels clicking and rumbling on the rails, feeling the interior motion as we traveled and watching the rural scenery passing right to left by my passenger compartment window in the fading light of dusk I played out in my imagination every thrust and parry the conversation might take. I knew I could not fail or else accept defeat and have to contemplate a much worse outcome to the war

At 6:15 p.m. I could feel the large black steam engine and the long train it was pulling starting to slow down and I heard the conductor's Yorkshire baritone voice in the passage way announce "Next stop Doncaster, all passengers for Doncaster disembark next stop."

Collecting my coat and hat as well as a hastily packed bag I made my way off of the passenger carriage and towards the station where I hoped that I could find suitable transportation to Holmes country residence. Seeing a lone motor taxi waiting almost as if the driver knew I was coming I climbed in and instructed the driver to take me to the "Beeches"

"The Beeches" as Holmes had described his retirement residence to me in a previous letter was as he had written. It was set back a short distance from the main road bordered by a small front lawn. The cottage was surrounded by a low black cast iron picket fence with green hedge behind the fence and both being about waist high. The two story residence itself was modest in terms of its length breadth and height.

The four large rectangular parlor latticed windows downstairs and the two smaller up stairs latticed windows of what I assumed was the main bed room faced the main road and were set in blue grey cobble stone that was capped by a thatched gable roof.

Set at ninety degrees to the right were two large latticed square windows also set in blue grey cobble stone and also capped by a thatched gable roof of which I took to be the dining area and the adjoining pantry.

As I opened the low black cast iron front gate to walk up the stone path to Holmes front door to announce my arrival I noticed that the front entrance was set in between the front and side of the cottage at an interesting forty five degree angle.

Noticing the absence of a proper brass door knocker I rapped three times on the green wooden door to let anyone inside know I was waiting to enter. Repeating this action one more time and not receiving a reply I decided to proceed about to the back of the cottage to see if anyone might be in the garden.

As I made my way around the cottage and started to see the property in back I noticed it was entirely carpeted in close cut grass without any signs of growing vegetation. The only thing "growing" were several white painted waist high structures which from the activity surrounding them I knew were bee hives.

Using elementary deduction (I had learned from my friend) I assumed that the tall appropriately attired individual standing in the middle of the collection of hives and blowing smoke onto the honey comb while extracting it, (Holmes had told me once this was done to calm the bees) could only be my friend.

"Holmes?" I stated to get his attention hopefully without unsettling him or his beekeeping activity. He placed the honey comb back in its slot, turned to me and removed the protective bonnet.

Looking at me with a mixture of both genuine surprise and joy he replied "Watson what an unexpected surprise. I didn't think that with your very busy schedule at the hospital you would have any time to board a train to come and visit with me." Looking at the bag in my handI was holding onto "much less stay for a visit."

I wished that I could share his joy at seeing me after a long time but remembering the things I had been made privilege to at my dining room table I simply stated "I have come about the telegram I sent you."

While he removed the protective gloves he recited the unanswered telegram from memory "...matter of gravest concern (stop) return to London a.s.a.p. (stop) have information that could potentially change outcome of the war (stop) Watson (stop).

"Watson if there is anything I have learned is that given enough time almost any difficulty will eventually work itself out. The present condition that the world finds itself in these days is too big and far too complicated for one person to try to address or remedy. Come let me show you my new residence."

Chapter 12

Holmes then led me from the back garden where his bee hives buzzing with activity to the inside of his cottage. As I surveyed the interior I was struck by the absence of all the things I had become familiar with at 221B Baker Street

Over the years Holmes had acquired an extensive collection of objects that defined who and what he was, where he had been and what he had done. Vanished was the thick oriental floor rug, the rich dark oak paneled walls, the ornately decorated plaster ceiling and the large framed picture of the Reichenbach Falls that had hung above his mantle. The mantle itself that had held many of Holmes trinkets and souvenirs (and some times loose pocket change) from some of his more interesting cases.

Absent was the hearth and coal scuttle beneath which kept Holmes rooms warm on cold winter days, the green leather chair and matching table with its coal oil lamp the very furniture which was where I had spent many happy hours making entries into my journal.

Also missing were the two upholstered brocade chairs the closest one to the hearth always being his favorite, the matching love seat where many of Holmes future clients had been invited to sit and unburden themselves in hopes that Holmes would take up their case.

Gone was his desk (where he kept his "solution) and chair, the book case, filing drawers and stacks of newspapers that Holmes always turned to when he needed a particular piece of information in connection to a difficult case. Probably most noticeably was the daily human pageantry typical of London that had entered into view from the three large windows facing onto Baker Street.

After he had shown me the downstairs and up stairs of his new dwelling, he asked two questions "have you eaten yet?" and "what time tonight does your train leave the Doncaster station to return to London?"

In turn my reply to both questions was, "No, not yet" and "Tomorrow morning at 9:00 a.m." Realizing he had reached something of an impasse Holmes calmly stated "Then I shall set the table for two and find somewhere you can comfortably sleep tonight."

While I sat at the table waiting to see what was for supper and unrealistically hoping that Mrs. Hudson would suddenly appear bearing one of her famous meals Holmes walked from the pantry to the table carrying what looked like a large white china soup tureen.

My look of facing the unexpected must have caught Holmes attention. To put me at ease while ladling some of the contents from the large serving dish into his bowl he assured me "It's a local dish made with rabbit, fresh vegetables and some spices. It's quite good." Here he paused to gauge my reaction.

Not receiving one he moved the tureen a little closer in my direction and handed me the ladle. Then knowing the next obvious question he smiled his representative smile and commented "As well as learning to care for bees Watson I have mastered the basic of cooking."

While enjoying Holmes some what rustic meal I realized that mere words were not going to be enough to persuade Holmes to return with me. Then I decided to use a similar approach to that which Einstein had used to explain his theory to Mary and me. Knowing my course of action I innocently started the dinner conversation much the same way as our guest had that night.

"How do we usually extract energy from a raw source?" Holmes also reasoning that this was only a rhetorical question answered "By burning coal or wood, compressing petrol in a cylinder then igniting it much as a motor car does, lighting a candle or gas lamp"…then added his own view "or by lighting the fuse to a stick of dynamite."

Now knowing I had engaged his attention I answered "The only problem with this is that it is inefficient. You never get the full potential of energy from the raw material being utilized."

Leaning forward a little Holmes said "Go on." To which I explained "A Swiss patent clerk has developed a theory that would allow you to achieve a very large amount of energy from a very small source."

Now very much like a blood hound that has caught the sent of its prey Holmes asked "The source?" "The source is the mineral uranium" I replied …"which in my medical practice I have some limited knowledge. I know that if it is handled for too long a person could develop what was known as radiation poisoning and eventually die. "

Knowing that I was going to have to end this persuasive discussion with a graphic demonstration I asked what types of vegetables or fruit he had in his larder. Mentally going through his inventory of fresh food, Holmes listed off "Some turnips, a few potatoes and a couple of tomatoes."

"Bring a bowl and the smallest tomatoes you have, I have a demonstration to show you. " Placing the bowel with its contents in front of me Holmes sat back down and watched. For drama I waited a bit then began. As I picked up the bright red fruit I stated "Let us say that this tomato, although certainly not to scale represents a small amount of uranium."

Here as Einstein had done I paused while Holmes mentally transformed the innocent vegetable into something more toxic and dangerous. "Now conventional wisdom would say that we can't by any means release the potential energy stored inside."

Seeing his skeptical reaction of something so relatively small containing any form of energy I assured him that there was more energy inside than could be imagined. "With a theory or process that Einstein calls nuclear fusion, which simply translated means that when a lot of pressure is equally applied to say this tomato watch what happens."

I placed the tomato back in the bowel and asked Holmes to stand next to me. It was at this point I slowly brought the palm of my hand down, we watched as the tomato went from being round to squat to bursting open thereby releasing the juice and seeds that had been stored inside.

Then while wiping my right hand clean I solemnly stated "Instead of dealing with the contents of what is sometimes thought of as both a fruit and vegetable and instead you should substitute uranium, you would have an explosive force of unimaginable power and life destroying devastation".

Holmes examined the damaged tomato in the bowl "Life is infinitely stranger than anything which the mind of man could invent. We would not dare to conceive the things which appear to be mere commonplaces of existence".

"If we could fly out of that window hand in hand, hover over this great city, gently remove the roofs, and peep in at the queer things which are going on; the strange coincidences, the planning's, the cross-purposes, the wonderful chains of events, working through generations, and leading to the most outré results, it would make all fiction with its conventionalities and foreseen conclusions most stale and unprofitable.

It is not so impossible, however, that a man should possess all knowledge which is likely to be useful to him in his work, and this, I will endeavor in my case to do. Is there any other point to which you would wish to draw my attention?" Shaking my head no Holmes asked a rhetorical question. "When does the train we must be on tomorrow morning to return to London leave Doncaster station?"

"I assume you knew ahead of time of my reaction to this demonstration and took the liberty of purchasing my return ticket?" Pulling Holmes railway ticket out of my inner coat pocket I announced "Our train leaves the station at 9:15 a.m. tomorrow morning." Boarding the London bound train at the Doncaster station the next morning Holmes profoundly stated "These are much deeper waters than I had thought."

Chapter 13

May 5. German airship "L.Z.-85" brought down by British gunfire at Salonika.

On the morning south bound trip back from Doncaster to London, Holmes had me relate all that I knew and had come to know about Einstein, his ideas and theories.

Of course already knowing about uranium and its potential as a weapon was the reason for our journey. It was when I gave the details of a series of "by chance" meetings that happened in Zurich between the patent clerk and a person by the name of Margaretha Geertruida "M'greet" Zelle, and the lady in question has been described as a dancer and an entertainer.

"If it turns out to be the same woman then I know her as Mata Hari. Fraulein Zelle adopted her stage name in 1905 in Paris when she started to win fame as an exotic dancer. She is a contemporary of dancers Isadora Duncan and Ruth St. Denis, leaders in the modern dance movement, which around the turn of the 20th century started to look to Asia and Egypt for artistic inspiration.

She poses as a Java princess of priestly Hindu birth, pretending to have been immersed in the art of sacred Indian dance since childhood".

"There is a dark side to her that Mr. Einstein may not be aware. Because the Netherlands remains neutral as a Dutch subject Margaretha Zelle is able to cross national borders freely. To avoid the battlefields, she travels between France and the Netherlands via Spain and Britain and her movements inevitably attract attention. In early 1916, she was travelling by steamer from Spain when her ship called at the English port of Falmouth".

"There she was arrested and brought to London where she was interrogated at length by Sir Basil Thomson, Assistant Commissioner at New Scotland Yard in charge of counter-espionage. He gave an account, alleging that she eventually admitted to working for French Intelligence. Initially detained in Canon Street police station, she was then released and stayed at the Savoy Hotel".

"It is unclear if she lied on this occasion, believing the story made her sound more intriguing, or, if French authorities were using her in such a way, but would not acknowledge her due to the embarrassment and international backlash it could cause.

The Netherlands remaining neutral during the armed conflict uncovered something of a paradox; it was heavily involved in the war. German general Count Schlieffen, who was Chief of the Imperial German General Staff had originally planned to invade the Netherlands while advancing into France in the original Schlieffen Plan.

This was changed by Schlieffen's successor Helmuth von Moltke the Younger in order to maintain Dutch neutrality. Later during the war this neutrality would prove essential to German survival until the blockade by Great Britain later in 1916, when the import of goods through the Netherlands would no longer be possible. However, the Dutch were able to continue to remain neutral during the war using their diplomacy and their ability to trade.

"The British blockade means they can't import food. So steadily the Germans find their rations being cut from a diet rich in animal fats they end up living on turnips"... a member of Parliament

Chapter 14

As our train slowly made its way into the glass ceilinged sun lit concourse of the rail terminal I looked over at my friend to see how he was handling the transition from quiet rural life back to busy war time urban life.

For the briefest time Holmes expression of wonderment on his face was not unlike like that of a small child who has been allowed to explore the most fantastic toy shop of all time. Then realizing what he had come back to the look of wonder dropped and was replaced with one of already defeated resignation

There was a great mix of lively, energetic and spirited train station related noises with animated matching fast paced colorful sights which greeted and then washed over Holmes and me as we exited our railway carriage onto the platform.

People and luggage of all sizes seemed to be bearing purposefully in various directions each to their respective rail passenger transport. Every once in awhile, there could be noticed above the great wave of sounds and sights the sharp piercing blast of a steam engine's whistle or the baritone voice of a conductor announcing to straggling last minute passengers "all aboard"

Orienting ourselves in the right direction we made our way out from the vast and busy rail way terminus and onto Euston Road in front of Kings Cross Station to flag a motor taxi that would take us both back to my home and my waiting wife.

After getting into the taxi together and giving the driver directions to our eventual destination I casually mentioned to Holmes "Of course you will stay with Mary and me until we have brought this case to an end." Our drive to 126 Hill House Road was a silent witness to the fact that that not anybody or anything even this far removed from the battlefields of Europe had escaped the ravages of the war.

May 7. Qasr-i-Shirin (Western Persia) occupied by Russian forces Serbian Government set up at Salonika. Life at our house had now adjusted to include our much beloved guest.

We had decided to spend the day yesterday getting caught up on the events that had come and gone in our respective lives. Mary showed a remarkable interest in all things related to bee keeping and was pleasantly amazed to learn that Holmes was now something of an accomplished cook.

Holmes in a less than convincing manner dismissed Mary's culinary compliments with "Not being in Mrs. Hudson's constant care and her attention it was a choice of either learning to cook even if it is only rudimentary in nature or starve."

May 9. British and French Governments conclude "Sykes-Picot" agreement as to eventual partition of Asia Minor

Chapter 15

Later after dinner when all three of us were comfortably seated in the parlor, Holmes and I were reading the evening edition of The Times while Mary was occupied with some needle point.

He suddenly folded the section he had been occupied with, dropped it beside his chair and said "Watson I have sifted through all the data I have acquired from you and Einstein. I have come to the conclusion that Mata Hari must to be stopped before she divulges what information we *think* she may be privileged to and would want to sell to some foreign government or hostile power".

After a brief pause he continued "It is of the highest importance in the art of detection to be able to recognize, out of a number of given facts, which are incidental and which vital. Otherwise my energy and attention will be dissipated instead of being concentrated."

Lowering my section of the paper to get a better view of him I asked with genuine concern in return "How will you bring this about?" Trying to get him to see the scale of the project I went on to state the obvious "Most of Europe is at war and I would think that it would be very difficult to travel easily or safely as a British subject".

"Watson in solving a problem of this sort, the grand thing is to be able to reason backward. Which can be a very useful accomplishment, and an easy one, but people do not practice it much. In the everyday affairs of life it is more useful to reason forward, and so the other tends to be neglected. There are fifty who can reason synthetically for one who can reason analytically."

Holmes beamed in a way to tell me he had already thought of an ingenious solution "Not as a British subject but rather as a naturalized Dutch citizen who was born in Sint Maarten." Thinking I could bring this unsafe and some what reckless plan to an end I exclaimed "But in order for this work Holmes you will need to be fluent in Dutch."

Holmes smiled his hallmark smile again and then sagely stated "What one man can invent, another can discover" he stood up from his chair and without hesitation spoke as if he had been born to the language…"Ik heb een het werk kennis van de Nederlandse taal sinds enige tijd gehad." "Which translates to" he continued "I have had a working knowledge of the Dutch language for some time.

Turning to my wife Holmes made a request that he knew she was better suited for. "Mary I will need your help in procuring suitable clothing that will reasonably pass for Dutch brick layers apparel."

Mary put down her needle point and considered for a moment. Then she said that she knew of a widow who would like to see her husband's clothes receive some use again. She then agreed to call and collect whatever Holmes thought he might need. Next sounding very much like someone ready for an expedition Holmes stated "all that is left to do is acquire the tools of my new trade and I will be ready."

Chapter 16

May 10. Agreement signed at Berlin re: employment of British and German prisoners of war.

Holmes convincingly finished displaying his knowledge of the European language by stating "Mijn naam is Pieter Joost en ik ben een metselaar" which translates to "my name is Pieter Joost and I am a brick layer" he then went on to add "Ik ben van Steenwijk in de Nederlandse provincie van Overijssel I am from Steenwijk in the Dutch province of OverIjssel"

Of course Holmes had not chosen this particular skill for mere intellectual stimulation or to occupy his time between cases. He had previously (along with a convincing disguise and dialec used this particular combination in the past. It was while he was working on a case searching for a very valuable set of coins.

The purloined and subsequently returned pieces were part of a private monetary collection. The obverse (face of the coins) of the 10 gold Florins 1875 issue showed a large portrait of King Willem III facing right. Above is the inscription (legend) GOD ZIJ MET ONS. Below is KONING WILLEM DE DERDE.

The reverse of the coins showed a crowned lion bearing a sword and arrows on a large shield surmounted by a large crown. At either side is the denomination 10 F. The 1875 reverse has the date 1875 at the top, and the legend KONINGRIJK DER NEDERLANDEN, running anticlockwise from 11 o'clock to 1 o'clock.

Although he was excellent at what he did Holmes continuously refuted his skills with disguise "It is always awkward doing business with an alias." It might be of some interest that this particular case was not among the 17 I had recorded and documented

"Watson we shall need a well thought out plan and course of action if we are to successfully locate Mata Hari and convince her not to exploit any of the information she may now own. Not entirely knowing the people and situations he was about to get involved with.

The many unknown risks my friend was about to under take to retrieve the information it was at this moment, hearing these words from Holmes that I had a premonition that somehow my personal and professional relationship with Holmes might be changed for the worse forever.

With the thought of potential loss in my mind I shook my head slightly from side to side, then with some small sadness in my voice I softly expressed my growing frustrations "This is why I hate this war, it puts demanding strains on people's personal and professional relationships and it also appears to test friendships as well as marriages."

Mary moved closer to me and took my hand in hers to assure me that our marriage was safe and secure. Holmes assessing the situation calmly stated "I ought to know by this time that when a fact appears to be opposed to a long train of deductions it invariably proves to be capable of bearing some other interpretation".

Holmes continued "It is an old maxim of mine that when you have excluded the impossible, whatever remains, however improbable, must be the truth. And what remains here is that when I meet the lady I alone will have to convince her to change her mind."

Knowing that he already had most of his plan in place I wondered how he was going to be able to locate and contact Mata Hari because the nature of her profession would mean that she would never be in one city or country for any great amount of time.

"I shall get in contact with a Thomas Quinlan a well known Impresario who will no doubt have knowledge of the exotic dancer's touring itinerary." Thomas Quinlan is the son of Dennis Quinlan, a railway clerk, and Ellen Quinlan, née Carroll. He is the eldest of five children.

Quinlan studied as a baritone and an accountant simultaneously. In 1901 he was company secretary of the Withnell Brick Company. He began music management in 1906, touring among others Enrico Caruso, Fritz Kreisler, John Philip Sousa and including a Nellie Melba tour of Ireland in 1908.

After visiting the entertainment producer, whose office was located at number 6, Harrowby Street, London, Holmes found out that Mata Hari would be on tour for the next 10 months from May of this year until February 1917. She would be performing on stage in most of the major cities in Europe as well as making special appearances in Baltimore, Maryland and Portland, Oregon in the United States.

May 14 agreement signed at London for transfer of British and German wounded and sick prisoners of war to Switzerland.

Over eight million men were incarcerated as prisoners of war in camps scattered across Europe and beyond, in Siberia, Turkey, Mesopotamia and parts of Africa. More than half were taken prisoner on the eastern Front.

Although there were differences across the host nations in the mortality rates and conditions, all the major belligerents adhered to the provisions regulating the treatment of prisoners of war laid out in the 1907 Hague Convention, which stated that all prisoners had to be treated humanly.

It also stipulated that the signatory countries should send relief to their imprisoned soldiers in the form of food parcels and clothing. While Austria Hungary made modest provisions, Germany and Britain were more generous.

Chapter 17

May 16, Second Military Service Bill extending compulsion to married men passes the British House of Commons. This bit of news meant that as a medical doctor, I was of course exempt from any military responsibility, but my obligation to the hospital now increased.

I had a feeling that the precious few minutes I had to spare with Mary and also documenting the daily telegrams and occasional letters from Holmes would leave me little time. I knew he would be sending back to London from the continent updating me on the events of the case.

With the clothes and tools of his trade and identity papers (I never queried him as to how he had obtained them, but knowing Holmes I thought best not to ask). I accompanied the now packed Holmes while he purchased his train ticket on the London, Chatham and Dover Railway.

The Chatham, as it is known, is much criticized for its often lamentable carriage stock and poor punctuality, but in two respects it is very good: it uses the highly effective Westinghouse brake on its passenger stock, and the Sykes 'Lock and Block' system of signaling. It has an excellent safety record.

Holmes trip to the continent would begin at the Ludgate Hill railway station. It is situated in London and was opened by the LC&DR as its City terminus on 1 June 1865. It is located on the Ludgate (railway) Viaduct between Queen Victoria Street and Ludgate Hill, slightly north of Blackfriars station.

His travel by rail would terminate at the Priory railway station being the main station in Dover in Kent. From Dover Holmes would board the English Channel ferry belonging to the London, Brighton and South Coast Railway (LB&SCR) named the Arundel for Calais France.

Chapter 18

May 17 with final strict and specific instructions as to how I was to record his daily dispatches Holmes was on his way from London to Dover then he would be on to Calais France. Later that day I received the first of many telegrams this one originated from Dover (via the Electrical and International Company)...Watson (stop) arrived Dover (stop) waiting to board channel ferry (stop) will contact you on arrival Calais (stop) Holmes (stop)

Early that evening I received notice from a messenger (via The Atlantic Telegraph Company formed in 1856) confirming Holmes had successfully crossed the English channel...Watson (stop) have arrived Calais (stop) boarding next train to Paris (stop) hope to make contact with MH at Lapin Agile (stop) Holmes (stop)

Anytime before the war a channel crossing would not have warranted any kind of communication. But it was the exceptional strategic importance of the Channel as a tool for blockade recognized by the First Sea Lord Admiral Fisher in the years before World War I.

"Five keys lock up the world! Singapore, the Cape, Alexandria, Gibraltar, Dover However on July 25, 1909 Louis Blériot successfully made the first Channel crossing from Calais to Dover in an airplane. Blériot's crossing signaled the end of the Channel as a barrier-moat for England against foreign enemies.

Because the Kaiserliche Marine *the Imperial German Navy* surface fleet could not match the British Grand Fleet, the Germans developed submarine warfare, which was to become a far greater threat to Britain. The Dover Patrol was set up just before war started to escort cross-Channel troopships and to prevent submarines from accessing the Channel, thereby obliging them to travel to the Atlantic via the much longer route around Scotland.

Paris...the cities way of life continued virtually the way it had until the eve of the outbreak of the First World War on 2 August 1914. Like other French cities, Paris initially welcomed the war as an opportunity to gain revenge for the defeat of 1870. Within a month, however, the city was full of refugees and the Germans were just 15 miles from the city. The government was evacuated to Bordeaux in the expectation that Paris would again fall to German forces.

The city was saved, however, by a desperate French effort to reinforce their lines and by a German failure to press home the attack. In the most famous incident of the "miracle on the Marne", as it became known, thousands of Parisian taxis were commandeered to carry soldiers to the front lines. The Germans were pushed back to the Oise some 75 miles away from the city.

Holmes kept an accurate account of his travel. Arrived unchallenged and unquestioned (as a Dutch brick layer) at Gare Saint Lazare at about 9:00 p.m. then took public under ground transportation (locally known as the **Métro**) from the train station **to the** Hotel Lutetia located at 45 Boulevard Raspail.

After registering as **Pieter Joost a brick layer from Steenwijk in the Dutch province of OverIjssel** and unpacking my one bag I decided to take in some of the social life this city of lights is famous for. It was a remarkable spectacle to see all of the city boulevards and the Café de Flore (an out door bistro lit over head by strings of small electric lights) it's self were surprisingly busy and bustling with evening clientele passing pedestrian and motoring Parisians.

Between the social interactions, food and drink being served and bits of pleasant conversations overheard at the brasserie, if I had not stopped to scan the newspaper "Le Figaro" that had been left by the previous patron of the table where I was sitting I would scarcely know there was a war being waged.

Nightfall has a way of hiding some of the terrible scars that war can inflict on such a beautiful city. January 29 Paris had been bombed by German zeppelins for the first time. As I was taking in the morning famous Parisian historic sites (without my disguise) there was still much evidence that this new type of warfare had taken place.

While touring the Louvre museum in the afternoon and appreciating the many paintings in its collection I hoped that the information I had received from Thomas Quinlan, the impresario, regarding Mata Hari's itinerary was correct and her scheduled appearance on the stage at Lapin Agile, a famous Montmartre cabaret would be at 8.00 p.m.

While taking in the museums collection of Hughes paintings I began composing a persuasive argument that might convince the lady to withhold the information she had and travel back to London with me. To create an air of respect and trust I had decided to meet and negotiate with Mata Hari as myself rather than as my alter ego, "the brick layer".

Lapin Agile is a famous Montmartre cabaret, at 22 Rue des Saules, 18th arrondissement of Paris, France. It was originally called "Cabaret des Assassins". Tradition relates that the cabaret received this name because a band of assassins broke in and killed the owner's son.

The cabaret was more than twenty years old when, in 1875, the artist Andre Gill painted the sign that was to suggest its permanent name. It was a picture of a rabbit jumping out of a saucepan, and residents began calling their neighborhood night-club "Le Lapin à Gill", meaning "Gill's rabbit".

Over time the name evolved into "Cabaret Au Lapin Agile", or, the Nimble Rabbit Cabaret. At the turn of the twentieth century, the Lapin Agile was a favorite spot for struggling artists and writers, including Picasso, Modigliani, Apollinaire, and Utrillo

The Lapin Agile, is located in the center of the Montmartre district in the 18th arrondissement of Paris, behind and slightly northwest of Sacre Coeur Basilica. Since this is the heart of artistic Paris at the turn of the twentieth century, there is much discussion at the cabaret about "the meaning of art".

Au Lapin Agile is also popular with questionable Montmartre characters including pimps, eccentrics, simple down-and-outers, a contingent of local anarchists, as well as, students from the Latin Quarter, all mixed with a sprinkling of well-heeled bourgeois out on a lark.

Many people visit the Lapin Agile, sitting at wooden tables where initials have been carved into the surfaces for decades. Located in a stone building on the steppe and cobbled Rue des Saules, the cabaret presents visitors with French songs dating back as far as the fifteenth century.

"Une table pour un monsieur?" the homme de porte asked and then guided me through the throng of wooden tables and seated patrons to an unoccupied one with a chair located near the stage. I was settled only long enough to quickly take in the smoky atmosphere and the regular clientele gathered in the crowded establishment who had also come to see Mata Hari.

I had my misgivings that espionage was being engaged in by all countries from the minute I had left Gare Saint Lazare and I felt that there was no reason why it should not be in practice at the Lapin Agile when an older Gallic appearing waiter wearing a full length white apron with a white towel draped over his left arm approached and asked above the din of conversation and eating "une certaine chose pour boire monsieur?"

"Un verre de Château Margaux S'il Vous Plaît" I replied, hoping my French accent was passible enough not to raise suspicions. As the ordered glass of wine was being placed on my table the house lights were dimmed, a single spotlight lit the stage and a slightly out of tune piano began playing introductory music.

The master of ceremonies (possibly also the proprietor) walked into the single spot light and began "mesdames et messieurs bonsoir actuellement je voudrais presenter" then someone offstage caught his attention because he paused momentarily, scanned the audience nodded slightly and continued "mesdames et messieurs que je suis au regret de vous informer que le mata hari indesposed et n'exécutera pas ce soir."

It struck me that by some means the lady had been informed of my presence and of my intentions while in Paris and had slipped my grasp. As a result of this development, my stay in Europe will be extended and tomorrow morning I board the train to Salzburg, Vienna.

Yours, Holmes

May 20. I was in the middle of my afternoon rounds at the hospital when I was told that there was a telegram waiting for me at reception. Watson (stop) unable to speak with MH (stop) may have been made aware of my presence (stop) travelling to Salzburg to persuade MH to return to London (stop) Holmes (stop)

May 31 Battle of Jutland begins...First British aerial co-operation with fleet in action. [British ships sunk - "Indefatigable", "Invincible", "Queen Mary", "Black Prince", "Defence" and "Warriror" German ships sunk - "Pommern", "Lützow", "Wiesbaden", "Rostock", "Frauenlob", "Elbing"]

The gap between expectation and reality was as great in the war at sea as in the war on land. The arms race in the decade before 1914 was dominated by rivalry over the construction of Dreadnoughts: fast, big gunned, heavily armored battle ships.

Germany had thirteen and was building seven more. Austria Hungary had three, America ten, Britain twenty. When Britain went to war, her people were led to believe that much of the fighting would be done at sea, where her navel superiority would guarantee a swift victory. Yet the war at sea did not turn out as expected.

"The all big gun battleship was in a sense the lineal descendant of Nelson's day. The idea of throwing a huge weight of metal over the greatest and destroying the enemy...War has changed. All that glamor is gone. It is now about logistics, survival, and protection of trade and defeating the enemy that way"...a sailor in the Royal navy

The set piece Battle of Jutland in 1916 was an exception, but though British losses were marginally greater, the result was that Germany's High Seas Fleet returned to its harbors and stayed there, preserved nearly intact as a negotiating counter for the war's end.

Instead, at sea, Germany would exploit the stealth and surprise afforded a new and almost untried weapon: the submarine. The sharpest minds in the Admiralties of both sides had long foreseen that submarines, fast patrol boats, mines and torpedoes could well dominate the coming conflict.

By striking at merchant ships, the submarine might also have a role in economic warfare, although one the British Admiralty was horrified at the thought: "Submarines are underhand, unfair and damned un English. As for U Boats attacking civilian ships, it is impossible and liners unthinkable. If they do, their captured crews should be hanged as pirates."

Not all Britain's admirals were that short sighted. Admiral Jackie Fisher realized "the submarine is the coming type of war vessel for sea fighting. It means that the whole foundation of our traditional naval strategy has broken down."

Two days into the war, Germany unleashed ten of its U Boats into the North Sea to hunt down the British fleet. One of them, U21, made her way into the Firth of Fourth, where the British cruiser HMS Pathfinder was leaving Rosyth naval base in Scotland.

U21 sunk her with a single torpedo and a new era of naval warfare had dawned. In time, Germany would not operate a policy of "all out" submarine warfare, in which, tiny merchant vessels or mighty ocean liners would be safe. The campaign would have a critical impact on the conduct and progress of war.

"If we are not to be finally bled to death full use must be made of the U boat as a means of war so as to grip England's vital nerve"...a U boat commander

Chapter 19

June 5. H.M.S. "Hampshire" sunk by mine off Scottish coast. Field Marshal Earl Kitchener and his staff drowned. - February 1917 The second revolution (after the Revolution of 1905) in the Russian Empire, this led to the collapse of the tsarist regime (Czar Nicholas II and the Empress Alexandra) and the inauguration of a democratic, republican government.

"The Tsar was a man who was very conscious of his own limitations. And his own limitations were considerable...He was much happier living the life of some kind of country gentleman"...a Russian field commander

Russia was weakened at the time by military failure, an economic crisis, and public discontent. The working class wanted better living and working conditions, the peasants wanted more land, and the oppressed nationalities wanted freedom. Almost everyone wanted an end to the war with the Central Powers

Due to the volume of letters and telegrams I received from June 1916 until February 1917 while Holmes was on the continent pursuing Mata Hari, rather than giving the reader a tedious and detailed day by day, month by month explanation of his detective investigations I will try to give an accurate (as far as I am able) abridged retelling of events that lead up to Holmes fateful return first to the Le Chat Noir then the Moulin Rouge Paris.

Before I continue, I must comment on the worrisome tone of some of Holmes letters. It gave me cause for concern and made me think that perhaps Holmes was starting to travel down a familiar road not unlike the one in the case of "*A Scandal in Bohemia*".

Perhaps he was starting to develop similar feelings for Mata Hari as he had for Irene Adler. I was hoping this was not true, I did not want Holmes keen dispassionate focus, sense of reason, deduction and justice to be clouded or lost by passing emotions.

To my friend she is always *the* woman. I have seldom heard him mention her under any other name. In his eyes she eclipses and absolutely dominates the whole of her sex. It was not that he felt any emotion akin to love for the lady.

All emotions and that one particularly, were abhorrent to his cold, precise but admirably balanced mind. He was, I take it, the most perfect reasoning and observing machine that the world has seen, but as a lover he would have placed himself in a false position.

He never spoke of the softer passions, save with a gibe and a sneer. They were admirable things for the observer — excellent for drawing the veil from men's motives and actions. But for those with trained intelligence to admit such intrusions into his own delicate and finely adjusted temperament was to introduce a distracting factor which might throw a doubt upon all his mental results.

Grit in a sensitive instrument, like a crack in one of his own high-powered lenses, would not be more disturbing than a strong emotion in a nature such as his. And yet, there was but one woman for him, and that woman was the late Irene Adler and Mata Hari, both of dubious and questionable memory.

Holmes long and circuitous trail of pursuit took him to such cities as Salzburg, Vienna, Amsterdam, Berlin, Rome, Barcelona, Milan, Madrid, Moscow, St. Petersburg and Krakow. The cabarets in each city he frequented (as Sherlock Holmes) without success were the Voltaire, Kleinkunstacademie (Cabaret Academy), Buntes Theater ("colorful theatre"), Zielony_Balonik (literally, *the Green Balloon*), The Butterfly Club, Cabaret Red Light and the Cabaret Paradis.

It was only when Mata Hari was to return to France at the first of February 1917; to perform at Le Chat Noir and at the Moulin Rouge that Holmes made a decision. In order to have any luck contacting her he would have to adopt his alter ego (at least in the form of correspondence) and approach her as a fellow Dutch citizen.

Le Chat Noir (French for "The Black Cat") was a 19th-century cabaret, meaning entertainment house, in the bohemian Montmartre district of Paris. It was first opened on 18 November, 1881 at 84 Boulevard Rochechouart by the impresario Rodolphe Salis.

It is thought to be the first modern cabaret: a nightclub where the patrons sat at tables and drank alcoholic beverages while being entertained by a variety show on stage, introduced by a master of ceremonies who interacted with people he knew at the tables

The Moulin Rouge opened October 6 1889, in the Jardin de Paris, at the foot of the Montmartre hill. Its creator Joseph Oller and his Manager Charles Zidler are formidable businessmen who understand perfectly the public's tastes. The aim is to allow the very rich to come and slum it in a fashionable district, Montmartre.

The extravagant setting – the garden is adorned with a gigantic elephant – allows people from all walks of life to mix. Workers, residents of the Place Blanche, artists, the middle classes, businessmen, elegant women and foreigners passing through Paris all rub shoulders.

When Holmes had taken a room and settled in at the Hotel Des Batignolles Paris, he composed and sent a note to Mata Hari who was to perform at the Le Chat Noir that evening.
11 februari Margaretha het is belangrijk dat ik met u over informatie spreek u uit kunt verkregen hebben kennis… zijn er ontzettende gevolgen als het in de verkeerde handen valt. Contacteer me bij het Hotel Des Batignolles 26 28 Rue Des Batignolles Pieter Joost

I am not fluent in Dutch but I believe Holmes note read *"February 11 Margaretha (being Mata Hari's first name) it is important that I speak with you about information you may have obtained from an acquaintance...there are dire consequences if it falls into the wrong hands." Contact me at the Hotel Des Batignolles 26 28 Rue Des Batignolles," Pieter Joost*

Chapter 20

Due to any number of reasons the note sent to Le Chat Noir went unanswered. Holmes, not wanting to attract any unnecessary attention to himself and posing as a Dutch citizen did not want to alert any foreign powers of Mata Hari's presence.

In Paris, he sent the same note (dated the 12) to her next performance venue The Moulin Rouge…her answer *Pieter I wlll komt vanavond u samen in mijn kleedkamer tijdens mijn avondmaalonderbreking bij 8:30 M*

Holmes entered the large and busy foyer of the Moulin Rouge at the prearranged time and asked the door man "quel chemin vers le vestiaire de Mata Hari's. The door man questioned " est la dame vous attendant?" Holmes produced the ladies note "la dame m'a envoyé cette note."

"Suivez-moi monsieur" the doorman then led Holmes through the double doors that led from the foyer to the main auditorium. The auditorium was vast it provided room for large musical numbers, as well as, a place for customers to dance between acts. The room also provided generous audience seating on each side.

As they moved towards the grand stage where acts were being advertised such as: 29 July, 1907: first appearance of Mistinguett on stage at the Moulin Rouge in the "Revue de la Femme". Her talent was immediately obvious. The following year she had a huge success with Max Dearly in "la Valse chaloupée

Turning to the right of the stage, both Holmes and the doorman entered a somewhat narrow wooden corridor, made even narrower by passing female performers. About halfway down the door man stopped in front of a particular door that was marked with a silver star and the name on the star read "Mata Hari."

The door man knocked and in response Holmes heard a female voice answer on the other side of the door answer "Oui?" "Un monsieur pour vous voir mademoiselle". "Come in Pieter"

When the lady turned to face her guest and Holmes entered the tiny dressing room there was a look of mutual surprise that passed between them. He for the somewhat revealing costume she was wearing, she for the fact that he was not dressed as a fellow Dutch citizen and therefore could not be Pieter Joost.

Turning back to face her dressing room table and mirror Mata Hari picked up the note she had just received and said "Mr. Holmes?" The next question she framed in a way as if she had no idea of the events that led up to Holmes appearance in her dressing room.

"Why is it so important that you have taken great pains to speak to me about information I may, or may not, have? Who is the acquaintance you speak of and what are the consequences of this information falling into the wrong hands?"

Not waiting for an invitation Holmes sat down on the closest chair and gave Mata Hari a summary of his meetings with Einstein and myself, going into great detail as to the where, why and gravity of the present situation.

Feigning interest in Holmes account she picked up her hand bag from the dressing table turned and faced Holmes. She smiled as she opened her hand bag pretending that she was looking for a precious article within.

"Mr. Holmes" she started as she changed her gaze from the imagined search of her bag to my friend "what a woman knows in her mind is the same as the contents of a woman's hand bag both are personal and private. She can choose where, when and with whom she desires to share them."

Holmes could see from her actions that it was vain to continue this course of action, for the young lady had decided with some determination not to tell her story, and it was evident that nothing short of force could get her to do so.

With Mata Hari's indifferent and somewhat laissez-faire answer, Holmes demeanor and attitude changed. Due to the urgency of the matter he pressed the subject "Mademoiselle it is important that I have an answer to my question."

Feeling that she had been boxed in Mata Hari's demeanor and attitude changed as well and then she shot back at him "You are Holmes, the meddler."

My friend smiled. "Holmes, the busybody!" His smile broadened. "Holmes, perhaps the Prefecture of Police Jack-in-office!" Holmes chuckled heartily.

Seeing no end to this battle of wits, Holmes humorous side faded and he replied with some seriousness "What you have done mademoiselle, or have not done in this world, may in the end be of little or no consequence."

"The question becomes what can you make people believe that you have done, or not done and are you willing to face the consequences of you believed actions?" The brief encounter ended with a back stage employee knocking on Mata Hari's door and announcing "cinq minutes jusqu'à ce que vous soyez sur la scène Mademoiselle."

Departing from the Moulin Rouge with what he thought of as rare certainty and conviction of the ladies guilt based on her actions Holmes knew what his next step would be.

The Prefecture of Police (*Préfecture de Police*), headed by the Prefect of Police (*Préfet de Police*), an agency of the Government of France (and part of the French National Police) which provides the police force for the city of Paris and the surrounding three suburban *départements* of Hauts-de-Seine, Seine-Saint-Denis, and Val-de-Marne.

It is also in charge of emergency services, such as the Paris Fire Brigade, and performs administrative duties, such as issuing identity papers and monitoring alien residents. The Prefecture of Police also has limited security duties in the wider Île-de-France *région*.

February 13. Mata Hari was arrested by Captaine Gustave Arnaud of The Prefecture of Police in her room at the Hotel Plaza Athénée in Paris. She was put on trial, accused of spying for Germany and consequently causing the deaths of at least 50,000 soldiers. Although the French and British intelligence suspected her of spying for Germany, neither could produce definite evidence against her.

Secret ink was found in her room, which was incriminating evidence at the time. She contended that it was part of her make-up. She wrote several letters to the Dutch Consul in Paris, claiming her innocence.

"My international connections are due of my work as a dancer, nothing else [...]. Because I really did not spy, it is terrible that I cannot defend myself." She was found guilty and was executed by firing squad on 15 October 1917, at the age of 41.

February 14. The British Government informs the Japanese Government that they will support Japanese claims to German possessions north of the Equator if it is understood that Japan will support similar British claims south of the Equator. British Government gives its pledge in the House of Commons that the restitution of Alsace-Lorraine is an object of the war.

Chapter 21

February 15. I received a telegram from Paris which I initially interpreted that the subject of Mata Hari had been resolved and that Holmes would soon be returning to London. The cable instead read. Watson (stop) have concluded the matter with MH now a issue for the police (stop) must return to my bees (stop) will write later with explanation (stop) Holmes (stop)

I didn't fully understand the nature of Holmes cryptic telegram until I picked up a copy of The Times at a news stand before returning home after a day at St Bartholomew's

And read this:

The Greatest Woman Spy of the Century tried and convicted of Espionage

Mata Hari, the archetype of the seductive female spy, is executed for espionage by a French firing squad at Vincennes outside of Paris.

She first came to Paris in 1905 and found fame as a performer of exotic Asian-inspired dances. She soon began touring all over Europe, telling the story of how she was born in a sacred Indian temple and taught ancient dances by a priestess who gave her the name Mata Hari, meaning "eye of the day" in Malay.

In reality, Mata Hari was born in a small town in northern Holland in 1876, and her real name was Margaretha Geertruida Zelle. She acquired her superficial knowledge of Indian and Javanese dances when she lived for several years in Malaysia with her former husband, who was a Scot in the Dutch colonial army. Regardless of her authenticity, she packed dance halls and opera houses from Russia to France, mostly because her show consisted of her slowly stripping nude.

She became a famous courtesan, and with the outbreak of World War I her catalogue of lovers began to include high-ranking military officers of various nationalities. In February 1917, French authorities on the direction of Mr. Sherlock Holmes, a London based consulting detective arrested her for espionage and imprisoned her at St. Lazare Prison in Paris.

In a military trial conducted in July, she was accused of revealing details of the Allies' new weapon, the tank, resulting in the deaths of thousands of soldiers. She was convicted and sentenced to death, and on October 15 she refused a blindfold and was shot to death by a firing squad at Vincennes.

Of course there is some evidence that Mata Hari acted as a German spy and for a time as a double agent for the French, but the Germans had written her off as an ineffective agent whose pillow talk had produced little intelligence of value.

Her military trial was riddled with bias and circumstantial evidence, and it is probable that French authorities trumped her up as "the greatest woman spy of the century" as a distraction for the huge losses the French army was suffering on the western front. Her only real crimes may have been an elaborate stage fallacy and a weakness for men in uniform

It should be noted here that Holmes had thoughtfully commented "Circumstantial evidence is a very tricky thing, it may seem to point very straight to one thing, but if you shift your own point of view a little, you may find it pointing in an equally uncompromising manner to something entirely different."

March 26. The first battle of Gaza British cavalry troops retreat after 17,000 Turks block their advance. It had almost been more than a month since I had any communication from Holmes. I was beginning to wonder how this whole affair had weighed on him and if he felt that in some way he alone was responsible for the death of the lady.

…I came away from the inside letter slot of our front door expecting to find among the collection of envelopes now in my left hand one in particular addressed from Holmes. I hoped that it may cast some light on a dark (for him) subject and possibly allowing publication of the anthology I had proposed to him.

Mary, coming to meet me sensed disappointment in my manner and acting upon the emotion now playing on my face stopped and stood in front of me, she lovingly reached out and took my right hand in hers looked me in the eyes then in a soothing voice said "John you know that Sherlock will answer your request in good time. "

"After all, you know that he will share what he wants to share and remember if he had not wanted you to document any of his cases he would have forbidden you from ever putting pencil to paper from the first. I imagine with what he has endured he will need some time to sort it all out.

"Give him time dear" she continued "I know he has not abandoned you and will give his permission for you to undertake your project." My reply and acknowledgement of her loving words and thoughts was to warmly smile, gently squeeze her hand and say" Ah my voice of calm and gentle reason."

April 2. U.S. President Woodrow Wilson asks the U.S. Congress for a declaration of war on Germany. April 12 Canadian troops win the Battle of Vimy Ridge.

April 26. America declared war on Germany after nearly three years of neutrality. President Wilson made his decision reluctantly. Two recent developments compounded the gradual shift towards war: the German declaration of unrestricted submarine warfare in February 1917; and the interception of a telegram which revealed Germany's hopes that Mexico would side with the Central Powers and invade the United States.

America joined the war as an associate power, with an army that in April 1917, consisted of only 287,000 officers and men. Within two months more than 9 million men registered for the first draft, although only 2 million of them would ever become part of the American Expeditionary Force in France. The pressure was to equip and train the new troops in time to help bring victory to the allies

German First Quartermaster General Ludendorff calculated that, despite America's entry into the war, its largely untrained Expeditionary Force would not be ready for combat for at least another year. At the end of 1917, prospects were good for Germany on many fronts. The Austro Hungarians had beaten back the Italian army 80 miles.

Vladimir Ilyich Lenin April 22, 1870 is a Russian Marxist revolutionary and communist politician who led the October Revolution of 1917. As leader of the Bolsheviks, he headed the Soviet state during its initial years (1917–1924), as it fought to establish control of Russia in the Russian Civil War and worked to create a socialist economic system.

As a politician, Lenin was a persuasive orator, as a political scientist his extensive theoretic and philosophical developments of Marxism produced Marxism–Leninism, the pragmatic Russian application of Marxism.

The Russian Bolshevik leader, Vladimir Ilyich Lenin, had declared a temporary armistice aiming to take Soviet Russia out of the war; peace negotiations were underway with Romania; and Serbia remained under German occupation.

When I asked them (the Russian troops) what they wanted now they said they did not want to fight any more and pleaded to be allowed to go home...and live in freedom...a Russian field commander

For all its failings and for all its problems, the Imperial Russian Army had to the end held down 160 German and Austrian divisions. These were now free to be released and the effect of this on the Allied war effort was absolutely devastating.

General Ludendorff would have to act quickly to secure victory by launching a major new offensive on the Western Front. "The Last Card", as it was referred to by the German High Command, would be Germany's final bid to break through Allied lines before the arrival of American troops from across the Atlantic

April 27. Just when I had given up all hope of hearing from my friend Mary holding an envelope in her hand announced as I was coming through our front door Saturday afternoon, that there was a letter addressed to us from Doncaster.

I opened the envelope and removed one folded piece of paper bearing Holmes distinctive hand writing…it read

Watson, Mary

I must first start by profoundly apologizing to you both for not returning to London after my time in Paris. As you have no doubt already read in the newspapers the eventual fate of Margaretha Geertruida "Margreet" Zelle or Mata Hari. You have known from past cases Watson, whenever I have handed over a criminal into the custody of the police there was never any doubt that I was serving the law and that this was the right action to take.

However, with the case of Mata Hari there will always be some doubt as to whether she was in fact a genuine German spy who could have caused great harm, or if in fact, because of her career, only believed that she was a spy and held the idea she was capable of extracting important secrets from the men who came into her life while she was an exotic entertainer. In either case, it's a wicked world when a clever woman turns her brain to what she may believe is a crime. That is the worst of all."

Once or twice in my career I feel that I have done more real harm by my discovery of the criminal than ever he or she had done by his or her crime. I thought I had learned caution now, and I should have rather played tricks with the law of the land than with my own conscience."

Do you know Watson that it is one of the curses of a mind with a turn like mine that I must look at everything with reference to my own special subject. You look at scattered houses, and you are impressed by their beauty. I look at them, and the only thought which comes to me is a feeling of their isolation and of the impunity with which crime may be committed there."

Conviction, clarity of thought, never having any doubt and a firm belief in ones skills and abilities these are the defining qualities of a good and effective consulting detective. I fear that as a result of my involvement with the lady I have lost the very things that made me who I was. I think my impaired skills would be better suited to less demanding clients, meaning of course my bees and their beehives

There is one piece of unfinished business that should be attended to. If there is some way to contact Mr. Einstein in Bern Switzerland please assure him that I did my best to retrieve what he had thought he had lost at the Café Odeon. But because I was never really sure that the lady who had introduced herself to him as Margaretha Geertruida "M'greet" Zelle ever in fact had this knowledge from the start. I can only grimly assume that if she ever owned such information that may have changed the course of the war it died with her when she was executed as a spy by firing squad.

Watson it was a pleasure to have known you as a friend, companion and biographer during our times together while solving cases and the times rooming together at 221 B Baker Street. Mary it was a pleasure to have met you even if not under the usual conditions. Then as if to finish his last letter on an upbeat note Holmes quipped *"It would brighten my declining years to see a German cruiser navigating the Solent according to the minefield plans which I have furnished."*

It was at this point of Holmes letter that a deep sadness suddenly washed over Mary and me. Echoing the words that were already forming in my mind Mary said "I don't believe we shall ever see him again.

"Watson I leave you with one last directive…you may go ahead with the project you had proposed to me last Christmas. When your extensive anthology of my cases is printed and bound please send me an autographed copy so that I have some small souvenir of my career."

Warmest regards to you both,

Holmes

When Mary and I read the last line of my friend's letter we both felt as if we were standing at the South Hampton docks in the late afternoon waving good bye. The ship that Holmes was departing on was slipping further away down the Thames and in the process diminishing with each passing minute...until it and Holmes, were only a memory.

The end

Chapter 22

Post script – 2012

The First World War was fought on a truly global scale, requiring unprecedented resources of manpower and supplies. Distant colonies of the belligerent empires provided millions of tons of food and raw materials for the war effort. Britain's largest colony, India alone provided 3.7 million tons, including wool, timber, raw silk, beef and tea as well as 70 million rounds of ammunition and 172, 815 pack animals and cows.

This was also the first war to involve large scale troop movements. Thousands of soldiers from around the world joined the European war effort. Volunteers and conscripts, they served as soldiers and laborers, nurses, porters and cooks. British troops included millions of soldiers from across the vast and diverse Empire.

1.4 million Indians, nearly 620,000 Canadians, over 416,000 Australians, more than 200,000 New Zealanders and 136, 070 South Africans. They fought across the man fronts of the war, in Palestine and Mesopotamia, in Africa, at Gallipoli and, in creasing numbers on the Western Front.

In 1916, Field Marshal Sir Douglas Haig requested that 21,000 laborers be recruited to fill the manpower shortage caused by casualties during World War I. As China was initially not a belligerent nation, her nationals were not allowed by their government to participate in the fighting - although the Chinese later declared war against Germany and Austria–Hungary, on 14 August 1917.

The scheme to recruit Chinese to serve as non-military personnel was pioneered by the French government. A contract to supply 50,000 laborers was agreed upon on 14 May 1916 and their first shipment left Tianjin for Dagu and Marseille in July 1916. The British government also signed an agreement with the Chinese authorities to supply laborers. The recruiting was launched by the War Committee in London in 1916 to form a Labor Corps of laborers from China to serve in France and to be known as the Chinese Labor Corps.

The Chinese Labor Corps comprised Chinese men who mostly came from Shandong Province, and to a lesser extent from Liaoning, Jilin, Jiangsu, Hubei, Hunan, Anhui and Gansu Provinces. The first transport ship carrying 1,088 laborers sailed from the main depot at Weihaiwei on 18 January 1917. The journey to France took 3 months.

A total of about 140,000 Chinese workers served on the Western Front during and after the War. Among them, 100,000 served in the British Chinese Labor Corps. About 40,000 served with the French forces, and hundreds of Chinese students served as translators.

By the end of 1917 there were 54,000 Chinese laborers with the Commonwealth forces in France and Belgium. In March the Admiralty declared itself no longer able to supply the ships for transport and the British government was obliged to bring recruitment to an end.

The men already serving in France completed their contracts. By the time of the Armistice, the Chinese Labor Corps numbered nearly 96,000, while 30,000 were working for the French. In May 1919, 80,000 Chinese Labor Corps were still at work.

The workers were tasked with carrying out essential work to support the frontline troops, such as building dugouts, repairing roads and railways, digging trenches and filling sandbags. Throughout the war, trade union pressure prevented the introduction of Chinese laborers to the British Isles. Sidney and Beatrice Webb suggested that the Chinese Labor Corps were restricted to carrying out menial unskilled labor due to pressure from British trade unions.

The workers saw firsthand that life in Europe was far from ideal, and reported this on their return to China after the war. Chinese intellectuals of the New Culture Movement looked on the CLC as a point of pride - Chen Duxiu, for instance, bragged that "while the sun does not set on the British Empire, neither does it set on Chinese workers abroad." But the ill treatment of these workers was added to the list of grievances against Britain.

We have seen real war in earnest now. It has been a terrible time but we remain unbeaten though exhausted, and the men are extraordinarily cheerful. It is heart breaking to think of the fine fellows who have gone under...a British soldier

State of the armies

The original British Expeditionary Force, six divisions strong at the start of the war, had been wiped out by the battles of 1914 and 1915. The bulk of the army was now made up of volunteers of the Territorial Force and Lord Kitchener's New Army, which had begun forming in August 1914.

The expansion demanded generals for the senior commands, so promotion came at a rapid pace and did not always reflect ability. Haig started the war as the commanding officer of British I Corps, then was promoted to command the British First Army and then the BEF, an army group eventually comprising sixty divisions in five armies. This vast increase in numbers diluted troop quality and undermined the confidence inexperienced commanders had in their men; this was especially true of Rawlinson.

Entertaining the Troops

A key element in the success or failure of any military endeavor is the morale of the troops. During the First World War it was realized that an important factor in morale was having a wide range of recreations available for the soldier on rest (approximately three-fifths of a soldier's overseas service was spent in the rear of the lines).

Faced with the grim reality of conflict, troops sought entertainment as a form of escape, in order to mentally survive and continue functioning effectively. The Second World War saw an even greater emphasis placed on recreation and entertainment as a result of this Great War experience.

Many of the entertainments available to service personnel were intended to remind the troops of home and its normal civilian pursuits, such as dances, parties, dinners, clubs and visits to other establishments providing familiar food and drinks. In this way troops made a connection with the home front and were reminded of what they were fighting for.

Sightseeing was also a popular form of entertainment and provided service personnel with the opportunity to visit places that they may otherwise have never been to. These activities included tours of the Holy Land, sightseeing in cities such as London, Paris, Rome and Cairo, and admission to the cricket at Lords or to the State Apartments at Windsor Castle.

Like humans everywhere, troops did what they could to make their lives and environment endurable. As J.G. Fuller says, they had "learned from long experience that it was better to concentrate on pleasures than hardships, that the best way to render tolerable the worst conditions was to make a joke of them, that moments of escape ...should be exploited to the full."

Expectations of war

World War One soldiers knew their king and country expected them to fight to the death. Such was the expectation of their military commanders, their political leaders and even their loved ones that there was no question that if mortal danger came, they should face it like men. It was the only way for good to triumph over evil.

But this conflict quickly became the most brutal war in history and not even the most seasoned serviceman was prepared for the scale of carnage that unfolded before him. For many the horror proved too much. Hundreds were unable to cope, many were driven insane and several simply ran away.

But the army could no more afford to carry cowards than it could traitors, and many of those who did flee faced instant retribution with a court martial and death by firing squad.

British and Commonwealth military command executed 306 of its own men during the Great War. Those shot brought such shame on their country that nearly a century on, their names still do not appear on official war memorials.

Military justice

British troops witnessed the annihilation of their friends on a daily basis. Most of the three million British troops soon knew they faced almost certain death on the battlefield. Day after day they would witness the annihilation of their friends, never knowing if or when they would be next.

On some occasions whole battalions were wiped out, leaving just a handful of confused, terrified men. But those who shirked their responsibility soon learned there was no way out of the horror - if they ran from German guns, they would be shot by British ones.

Private Thomas Highgate was the first to suffer such military justice. Unable to bear the carnage of 7,800 British troops at the Battle of Mons, he had fled and hidden in a barn. He was undefended at his trial because all his comrades from the Royal West Kents had been killed, injured, or captured. Just 35 days into the war, Private Highgate was executed at the age of 17.

Many similar stories followed, among them that of 16-year-old Herbert Burden, who had lied that he was two years older so he could join the Northumberland Fusiliers. Ten months later, he was court-martialled for fleeing after seeing his friends massacred at the battlefield of Bellwarde Ridge. He faced the firing squad still officially too young to be in his regiment.

To their far-off generals, the soldiers' executions served a dual purpose - to punish the deserters and to dispel similar ideas in their comrades. Courts martial were anxious to make an example and those on trial and could expect little support from medical officers. One such doctor later recalled, 'I went to the trial determined to give him no help, for I detest his type - I really hoped he would be shot.'

Those condemned to death usually had their sentences confirmed by Field Marshal Sir Douglas Haig on the evening following their court-martial. A chaplain was dispatched to spend the night in the cell with the condemned man and execution took place the following dawn, with some men facing their last moments drugged with morphine or alcohol.

When the time came, the offender was tied to a stake, a medical officer placed a piece of white cloth over the man's heart and a priest prayed for him. Then the firing line - usually made up of six soldiers - was given orders to shoot. One round was routinely blank and no soldier could be sure he had fired a fatal shot.

Immediately after the shooting, the medical officer would examine the man. If he was still alive, the officer in charge would finish him off with a revolver.

Female spies

While women are still officially not allowed in combat in almost all nations, there is a long history of female involvement in warfare, even in ancient times. Espionage knows no gender and in fact being female could provide less suspicion and a better cover. There is extensive documentation of the role of women undercover and otherwise involved in intelligence work in the two world wars and some very interesting characters emerge from those two conflicts.

We have been introduced to one famous or infamous spy Mata Hari. While there is little doubt about Mata Hari's life as a stripper and a sometimes prostitute, there is actually some controversy about whether she was ever actually a spy. Famous as she was, if she was a spy she was fairly inept at it, and she was caught as the result of an informant and executed by France as a spy. It later became known that her accuser was himself a German spy and that her real role was in doubt. Likely she is remembered both for being executed and for having a memorable name and profession.

Another spy famous from World War I was also executed as a spy. Her name was Edith Cavell and she was born in England and was a nurse by profession. She was working in a nursing school in Belgium when the war erupted and although she was not a spy as we generally see them, she worked undercover to help soldiers from France, England and Belgium escape from the Germans.

At first she was allowed to continue as matron of a hospital and, while doing so, helped at least 200 more soldiers to escape. When the Germans realized what was happening she was put on trial for harboring foreign soldiers rather than for espionage and convicted in two days. She was killed by a firing squad in October of 1915 and buried near the execution site despite appeals from the United States and Spain.

When the Great War was finally ended through an agreed cease fire (I feel through an unfair arbitrary and forced armistice) on November 11 at 11:00 a.m. in 1918 the whole world breathed a sigh of relief. We truly thought that this would be the war to end all wars.

It wasn't until the terms and conditions of an unrealistic surrender and reparations that was forced on Germany at the treaty talks being held in Paris 1919 that the world would erupt into another world war only 21 years later.

Large sections of Germany's population refused to believe that their country had been defeated on the battle field. Rumors had spread that sabotage by traitors, pacifists and revolutionaries had lead to the German army's failure to secure a victory. And what Germany termed "the unheard of injustice of the peace conditions" resulted in the delay of their final acceptance of the Paris Peace Treaty.

The Armistice

The British public was notified of the armistice by a subjoined official communiqué issued from the Press Bureau at 10:20 a.m., when David Lloyd George, the British Prime Minister, announced:

"The armistice was signed at five o'clock this morning, and hostilities are to cease on all fronts at 11 a.m. to-day."[13] An official communique was published by the United States at 2:30 p.m.: "In accordance with the terms of the Armistice, hostilities on the fronts of the American armies were suspended at eleven o'clock this morning."[14]

News of the armistice being signed was officially announced towards 9 a.m. in Paris. One hour later, Foch, accompanied by a British admiral, presented himself at the Ministry of War, where he was immediately received by Georges Clemenceau, the Prime Minister of France.

At 10:50 a.m., Foch issued this general order: "Hostilities will cease on the whole front as from November 11 at 11 o'clock French time The Allied troops will not, until further order, go beyond the line reached on that date and at that hour."

Five minutes later, Clemenceau, Foch and the British admiral went to the Élysée Palace. At the first shot fired from the Eiffel Tower, the Ministry of War and the Élysée Palace displayed flags, while bells around Paris rang. Five hundred students gathered in front of the Ministry and called upon Clemenceau, who appeared on the balcony.

Clemenceau exclaimed "Vive la France!"—the crowd echoed him. At 11:00 a.m., the first peace-gunshot was fired from Fort Mont-Valérien, which told the population of Paris that the armistice was concluded, but the population was already aware of it from official circles and newspapers. The peace between the Allies and Germany would subsequently be settled in 1919, by the Paris Peace Conference, and the Treaty of Versailles that same year.

Last casualties

The news was quickly given to the armies during the morning of 11 November, but even after hearing that the armistice was due to start at 11:00 a.m., intense warfare continued right until the last minute.

Many artillery units continued to fire on German targets to avoid having to haul away their spare ammunition. The Allies also wished to ensure that, should fighting restart, they would be in the most favorable position. Consequently there were 10,944 casualties of which 2,738 men died on the last day of the war.

Augustin Trébuchon was the last Frenchman to die when he was shot on his way to tell fellow soldiers that hot soup would be served after the ceasefire. He was killed at 10:45 a.m. The last soldier from the UK to die, George Edwin Ellison of the 5th Royal Irish Lancers, was killed earlier that morning at around 9:30 a.m. while scouting on the outskirts of Mons, Belgium.

The final Canadian, and Commonwealth, soldier to die, Private George Lawrence Price, was killed just two minutes before the armistice to the north of Mons at 10:58 a.m., to be recognized as one of the last killed with a monument to his name.

And finally, American Henry Gunther is generally recognized as the last soldier killed in action in World War I. He was killed 60 seconds before the armistice came into force while charging astonished German troops who were aware the Armistice was nearly upon them.

The last reported German casualty occurred after the 11 a.m. armistice. A Lieutenant Tomas, in the Meuse-Argonne sector, went to inform approaching American soldiers that he and his men would be vacating houses that they had been using as billets. However, he was shot by soldiers who had not been told about the ceasefire

The German delegation while staying in Paris did not actually participate and was not a contributing party in the talks, but was rather told that they would be summoned and only at that time would they be made aware of the terms of the treaty that France, Great Britain and America had arbitrarily agreed to and that there would be no negotiations.

The reluctant acceptance drafted by a second German delegation (the first one having left in protest over their treatment and poor living accommodations) arrived barely ninety minutes before the Allied dead line, which if not endorsed (as drafted) threatened a resumption of the hostilities. The treaty was signed in the Hall of Mirrors at Versailles on 28 of June 1919 exactly five years to the day since the Sarajevo assassination.

If I were the Germans I shouldn't sign for a moment. You see it gives them no hope whatsoever, either now or in the future...a British diplomat to the 1919 Paris peace talks

In the end the Treaty of Versailles (and French demands) would have lasting repercussions. Dissatisfied European nations would be at the mercy of those seeking a military solution to avenge defeat or to make up for insufficient gains.

th in 14 years the Nationalist Socialist German Workers Party (N.S.D.A.P.) and its leader Adolph Hitler would come to power as a result of the social and economic turmoil of the terms of 1919 Paris Treaty and in 1933 form a one party government in Germany. Hitler's (and the N.S.D.A.P.) goal was to undo the restrictions and humiliation that had been imposed on Germany as a result of the treaty and restore the nation to its former glory.

It would take another horrifying global war to lay some of these ghosts to rest, yet the legacy of the First World War would continue to cast a shadow over the rest of the 20th century.

Chapter 23

Some notes at the end of the story...in no particular order

Pastiche

A pastiche is a literary or other artistic genre or technique that is a "hodge-podge" or imitation. The word is also a linguistic term used to describe an early stage in the development of a pidgin language.

In this usage, a work is called a *pastiche* if it is *cobbled together* in imitation of several original works. As the Oxford English Dictionary puts it, a pastiche in this sense is "a medley of various ingredients; a hotchpotch, farrago, jumble." This meaning accords with etymology: pastiche is the French version of the Greco-Roman dish pastitsio or *pasticcio*, a kind of pie made of many different ingredients.

The term denotes a literary technique employing a generally light-hearted tongue-in-cheek imitation of another's style; although jocular, it is usually respectful. For example, many stories featuring Sherlock Holmes, originally created by Arthur Conan Doyle, have been written as pastiches since the author's time.

Sherlock Holmes and the Terrible Secret was written in very much in the style and manner of my first Novella Sherlock Holmes and The Discarded Cigarette (both as a pastiche).

Again I have taken two historical fictional characters, Holmes and Watson and brought them together with two real historical figures Albert Einstein and Margaretha Geertruida "M'greet" Zelle better known as Mata Hari and set their story against the back drop of the history and day to day facts of world war one.

Before going on I should note that I set out originally only to write a story based in world war one, but as I was doing research I found out I didn't know as much about the basis of the war and it's impact on the people who were caught up in it.

With the fact that there are no longer any surviving veterans from the first world war…this global conflict has become the forgotten war…so now Sherlock Holmes and the Terrible Secret has become as much a story and a history lesson.

I should clear up one point in the story here although the two (Einstein and Mata Hari) meet at the Odeon café in Zurich whether by clever planning, chance or by serendipity in real life there was little chance that they would have exchanged names much less shared a lunch together.

I have departed from the usual Sherlock Holmes formula on a couple of points, first the period the story was set in 1914 – 1917, the use of modern (at the time) technology the motor car, telegrams and the telephone.

I have always felt that Mary Watson (Dr. John H. Watson's wife) had always been a minor one dimensional character and felt it was time to make her a real part of the story. The major departure on this point was in using Holmes first name as part of the story. This was mentioned early in the story and how it came about was mentioned later.

Holmes always comes off as unemotional cold and distant, I wanted to show a warmer and more human side to him by having Mary Watson address him and refer to him as "Sherlock" and him addressing her as "Mary." With the exception of Irene Adler in A Scandal in Bohemia and his brother Mycroft nobody (as far as I know) is recorded in any of Sir Arthur Conan Doyle's as using Holmes first name.

The one thing about writing fiction is that the writer can evoke artistic license…the process of fusion and its dangerous potential Einstein first explains to John and Mary Watson…then Watson explains to Holmes was actually discovered in the 1930's. At the time the story was set in Albert Einstein was in fact only a patent clerk.

On the eve of World War II, he (Albert Einstein) helped alert President Franklin D. Roosevelt that Germany might be developing an atomic weapon, and recommended that the U.S. begin similar research; this eventually led to what would become the Manhattan Project. Einstein was in support of defending the Allied forces, but largely denounced using the new discovery of nuclear fission as a weapon.

While writing the Terrible Secret I had to wonder how the world would have changed and even if there would ever have been a second world war if Germany had the knowledge of nuclear fusion and had built an atomic bomb to bring an end to the conflict.

Like Sir Arthur Conan Doyle in Sherlock Holmes in the Final Problem I have finished off Holmes not by sending him over a water fall but by sending him into self induced retirement. I don't believe he could continue to practice as a consulting Detective while wondering if he may have caused the death of a delusional woman

Three of Holmes cases mentioned throughout the story they are:

The Sign of the Four (1890), also called The Sign of Four, is the second novel featuring Sherlock Holmes written by Sir Arthur Conan Doyle. Doyle wrote four novels and 56 stories starring the fictional detective.

The story is set in 1887. The Sign of the Four has a complex plot involving service in East India Company, India, the Indian Rebellion of 1857, a stolen treasure, and a secret pact among four convicts ("the Four" of the title) and two corrupt prison guards. It presents the detective's drug habit and humanizes him in a way that had not been done in A Study in Scarlet. It also introduces Doctor Watson's future wife, Mary Morstan.

A Study in Scarlet is a detective mystery novel written by Sir Arthur Conan Doyle, introducing his new character of Sherlock Holmes, who later became one of the most famous literary detective characters. He wrote the story in 1886, and it was published the next year.

The book's title derives from a speech given by Holmes to his sidekick Doctor Watson on the nature of his work, in which he describes the story's murder investigation as his "study in scarlet": "There's the scarlet thread of murder running through the colorless skein of life, and our duty is to unravel it, and isolate it, and expose every inch of it."

"A Scandal in Bohemia" was the first of Arthur Conan Doyle's 56 Sherlock Holmes short stories to be published in *The Strand Magazine* and the first Sherlock Holmes story illustrated by Sidney Paget. (Two of the four Sherlock Holmes novels – *A Study in Scarlet* and *The Sign of the Four* – preceded the short story cycle). Doyle ranked "A Scandal in Bohemia" fifth in his list of his twelve favorite Holmes stories.

While the currently-married Dr. Watson is paying Holmes a visit, Holmes is called upon by a masked gentleman introducing himself as Count Von Kramm, an agent for a wealthy client. However, Holmes quickly deduces that he is in fact Wilhelm Gottsreich Sigismond von Ormstein, Grand Duke of Cassel-Felstein and the hereditary King of Bohemia. The King admits this, tearing off his mask.

It transpires that the King is to become engaged to Clotilde Lothman von Saxe-Meiningen, a young Scandinavian princess, but the King's in-laws-to-be would not allow the marriage should any evidence of his former liaison with an American opera singer, Irene Adler, be revealed to them. Adler herself is threatening to reveal the relationship upon the announcement of the King's betrothal by sending a photograph of the King (then the Crown Prince) and Adler together to the newspapers. The King's agents have tried to recover the photograph through sometimes-forceful means.

In Flanders fields the poppies blow

Between the crosses, row on row,

That mark our place; and in the sky

The larks, still bravely singing, fly

Scarce heard amid the guns below.

We are the Dead. Short days ago

We lived, felt dawn, saw sunset glow,

Loved and were loved, and now we lie,

In Flanders fields.

Take up our quarrel with the foe:

To you from failing hands we throw

The torch; be yours to hold it high.

If ye break faith with us who die

We shall not sleep, though poppies grow

In Flanders fields.

"In Flanders Fields" is a war poem in the form of a rondeau,(a rondeau plural rondeaux is a form of French poetry with 15 lines written on two rhymes, as well as a corresponding musical form developed to set this characteristic verse structure) written during the First World War by Canadian physician and Lieutenant Colonel John McCrae.

He was inspired to write it on May 3, 1915, after presiding over the funeral of friend and fellow soldier Alexis Helmer, who died during the Second Battle of Ypres. According to tradition, McCrae was initially unsatisfied with his work and discarded it, only to be retrieved by fellow soldiers.

McCrae fought in the second battle of Ypres in the Flanders region of Belgium where the German army launched one of the first chemical attacks in the history of war. They attacked the Canadian position with chlorine gas on April 22, 1915, but were unable to break through the Canadian line which held for over two weeks.

In a letter written to his mother, McCrae described the battle as a "nightmare": "For seventeen days and seventeen nights none of us have had our clothes off, nor our boots even, except occasionally. In all that time while I was awake, gunfire and rifle fire never ceased for sixty seconds.....

And behind it all was the constant background of the sights of the dead, the wounded, the maimed, and a terrible anxiety lest the line should give way."

Alexis Helmer, a close friend, was killed during the battle on May 2. McCrae performed the burial service himself, at which time he noted how poppies quickly grew around the graves of those who died at Ypres. The next day, he composed the poem while sitting in the back of an ambulance.

The story Sherlock Holmes and The Terrible Secret

would not have been possible without the diligent,

expert and professional work of my editor:

Thanks Dianne:

For your effort and time:

A job well done and a story that I can be proud to have
people read.

Dedication:

Thank you to everyone who has read, enjoyed and supported me with my first story *Sherlock Holmes and The Discarded Cigarette*. I hope you will enjoy reading my second story *Sherlock Holmes and The Terrible Secret* as much and I appreciate your continued support.

Also From Fred Thursfield

London 1895. A well known author, a theoretical invention
made real, and the importance of a sometimes overlooked clue
challenge Holmes and Watson to prevent the perfect crime.

Also From MX Publishing

Winners of the 2011 Howlett Literary Award (Sherlock Holmes book of the year) for '**The Norwood Author**'

From one of the world's largest Sherlock Holmes publishers dozens of new novels from the top Holmes authors.

www.mxpublishing.com

Including our bestselling short story collections 'Lost Stories of Sherlock Holmes' and 'The Outstanding Mysteries of Sherlock Holmes'.

New in 2012 [Novels unless stated]:

Sherlock Holmes and the Plague of Dracula
Sherlock Holmes and The Adventure of The Jacobite Rose [Play]
Sherlock Holmes and The Whitechapel Vampire
Holmes Sweet Holmes
The Detective and The Woman: A Novel of Sherlock Holmes
Sherlock Holmes Tales From The Stranger's Room
The Sherlock Holmes Who's Who
Sherlock Holmes and The Dead Boer at Scotney Castle
A Professor Reflects on Sherlock Holmes [Essay Collection]
Sherlock Holmes of The Lyme Regis Legacy
Sherlock Holmes and The Discarded Cigarette [Short Novel]
Sherlock Holmes On The Air [Radio Plays]
Sherlock Holmes and The Murder at Lodore Falls

Also from MX Publishing

Sherlock Holmes and The Lyme Regis Horror and the sequel
Sherlock Holmes and The Lyme Regis Legacy

Sherlock Holmes – Tales from the Stranger's Room
An eclectic collection of writings from twenty Holmes writers.

www.mxpublishing.com

186

Also from MX Publishing

Sherlock Holmes Travel Guides

London   Devon

In ebook (stunning on the iPad) an interactive guide to London

400 locations linked to Google Street View.

Also from MX Publishing

Sherlock Holmes Fiction

Short fiction (Russian Chessboard), modern novels (No Police Like Holmes), a female Sherlock Holmes (My Dear Watson) and the adventures of Mrs Watson (Sign of Fear, and Study in Crimson).

Also from MX Publishing

Biographies of Arthur Conan Doyle

The Norwood Author. Winner of the 2011 Howlett Literary Award (Sherlock Holmes Book of the year) and the most important historical Holmes book of this year 'An Entirely New Country'

Also from MX Publishing

Cross over fiction featuring great villans from history

  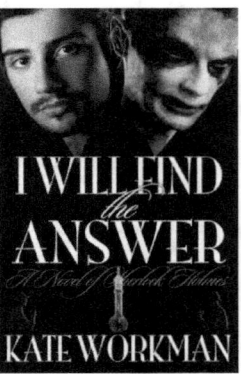

and military history Holmes thrillers

 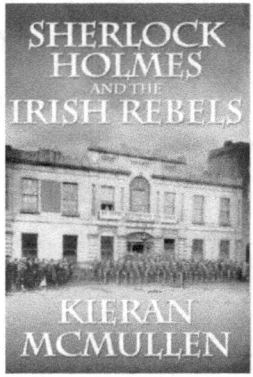

Also from MX Publishing

Fantasy Sherlock Holmes

And epic novels

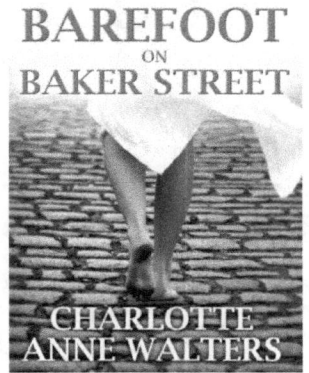